Joseph Roth, from a cigarette card, *c.* 1930

ABOUT THE TRANSLATOR

Richard Panchyk is the author, editor or translator of eighteen books, including *World War II for Kids*, *German New York City*, *Forgotten Tales of Long Island* and *Keys to American History*, as well as a study on Jewish assimilation and name change in the Austrian Empire during the nineteenth century. He is distantly related to Joseph Roth.

Also by Joseph Roth and available from Peter Owen

Flight Without End
The Silent Prophet
Weights and Measures

Joseph Roth

THE ANTICHRIST

Translated from the German and with an Introduction by
Richard Panchyk

Peter Owen
London and Chester Springs, PA, USA

PETER OWEN PUBLISHERS
73 Kenway Road, London SW5 0RE

Peter Owen books are distributed in the USA by
Dufour Editions Inc., Chester Springs, PA 19425-0007

Translated from the German
Der Antichrist
First published in 1934 by Verlag Allert de Lange, Amsterdam

This translation first published in Great Britain by
Peter Owen Publishers 2010
Translation © Richard Panchyk 2010
Introduction © Richard Panchyk 2010

All Rights Reserved.
No part of this publication may be reproduced
in any form or by any means without the prior
permission of the publishers.

ISBN 978-0-7206-1331-5

A catalogue record for this book is available from
the British Library

Printed and bound in Great Britain by
CPI Bookmarque Ltd, Croydon, Surrey CR0 4TD

The editor and publisher acknowledge their gratitude to
Williams Verlag for permission to quote from the works
of Stefan Zweig and to Gabriel Picard for permission to quote
from the works of Max Picard.

Contents

INTRODUCTION

I do not think that man can save man. I am a believer: man cannot
be saved except by Heaven. – Joseph Roth

The prodigious output of Joseph Roth (1894–1939) included
numerous novels, novellas, short stories and newspaper articles in
the space of only sixteen years between 1923 and 1939. While
much of Roth's fascinating oeuvre has been made available to
the English-speaking world in recent years, *Der Antichrist* (*The
Antichrist*) has remained out of print in English for seventy years.
This is unfortunate because, although it is perhaps his least-
known work it is also one of his most interesting, certainly his most
intense and densely packed, offering, as it does, valuable insight
into the persona of Joseph Roth.

Born Moses Joseph Roth of Jewish parentage in the town of
Brody, Galicia, in the Austro-Hungarian Empire (present-day
Ukraine), about eighty-seven kilometres (fifty-four miles) north-east
of present-day Lviv (then called Lemberg), Roth's own accounts of
his background were often misleading. He claimed to have been
born in a town called Svaby to a Christian father and Jewish mother.
In one 1934 interview he said his mother was a 'Russian Jew
always close to the ghetto' and his father a Viennese employed by
the Minister of Finance, an amateur artist, painter, sceptic and
alcoholic who died before Roth was even born. In truth, both

parents were Galician Jews; and the mentally unbalanced Nachum Roth left under the spell of a so-called 'wonder rabbi' even before Joseph was born and died in 1910. Joseph was raised by his mother and her relatives, although in adulthood he was friendly with some members of his father's family.

Just as fact and fiction are confused in Roth's telling of his own story, so they are commingled in *The Antichrist*. Is it a novel or a work of non-fiction? At first glance one may be inclined to call it non-fiction, a series of interconnected essays – it is true that some of the material is more or less recycled from Roth's non-fiction, articles he wrote during the 1920s and early 1930s. For example, the chapter on oil drilling is apparently based on a 1928 article he wrote about oil wells in Poland for the *Frankfurter Zeitung*. However, whatever of his own earlier journalistic work Roth borrowed here, he rewrote, refocused and fictionalized for use in *The Antichrist*. Although it has not typically been classified as fiction, Roth himself referred to *The Antichrist* as a novel. The most fictional aspect of the work is certainly the narrator's trip to Hollywood; Roth never set foot in the United States.

When compared to Roth's non-fiction, such as *The Wandering Jews* or the series of brief newspaper sketches (known in French as *feuilletons*) that have since been compiled and published as *What I Saw: Reports from Berlin* and *Reports from a Parisian Paradise*, it becomes clear that *The Antichrist* is more novel than essay, although it may more realistically be seen as a hybrid of the two genres. While it is ostensibly a work of fiction, *The Antichrist* may also be the closest thing to autobiography that Roth ever wrote.

The Antichrist is like nothing else in Roth's canon. It is more overtly political, more dogmatic, more thematically broad, more emotionally charged and more blatantly cynical than either his other novels or his non-fiction. The reviews for *The Antichrist* were mixed but were consistent in their agreement that the book was unique. The *New York Times* liked it; the British critic Frank Swinnerton found Roth's take on Hollywood 'bewildering'; the *Wiener Zeitung* called it a 'prophetical treatise' with 'apocalyptic' scenes; and a French review called it 'one of the most vehement protests of human conscience against that which reduces and destroys it'.

The 'vehement protests' in *The Antichrist* present Joseph Roth in a raw state, stripped bare of any pretensions, with the more intricate plots of his other books sacrificed here for the sake of message. The book's focus is trained on Roth's present – the state of the world between the outbreak of the First World War in 1914 and the Nazis coming to power in Germany in 1933, one of the most fateful periods in human history. Everything that 'reduces and destroys' human conscience is traceable to the Antichrist, whose long-expected arrival in the world has finally come during the early twentieth century.

Of course, the whole concept of the Antichrist as a theme for a Joseph Roth book is especially interesting considering Roth's Jewish background. Although his Jewishness was largely concealed in his writing, and he attempted to mask it or minimize it when asked about his background, neither was he a true convert to Christianity. He tried to identify himself with Catholicism at times, yet some of his books were heavily infused with Jewish sensibilities and culture, depicted through sympathetic characters. Joseph Roth, like many European Jews of the early twentieth century, could not simply be pigeon-holed into a particular religion. He sought to be treated as an assimilated citizen of the Austro-Hungarian Empire rather than as a member of a particular religion.

As usual with his books, Roth's various life experiences – as university student, journalist, soldier, traveller, philosopher and

Catholic-leaning Jew – inform much of *The Antichrist*. It is his extensive experience as a journalist that may well be the single strongest influence on all his fiction. Roth's urge to expose the multiple layers of truth on any given subject seems to be a driving force behind all of his writing. And, after all, any writer emerging from the confusion of the crumbling Austro-Hungarian Empire after the First World War had to confront and then reconcile multiple identities and alternate truths.

Roth expressed complexities of social reality through his carefully chosen words. His novels are characterized by a knack for capturing details and painting verbal pictures that themselves serve as his pointed commentary. His novels are replete with attention paid to details such as the sound of rainfall, the croaking of frogs or the stultifying atmosphere of a stuffy room. Many of these descriptions ring true not only because they capture an essence but because they are the *right* details, the sounds or sights that we as readers need described. Roth saw with the eyes we as readers wish to have; he answers our questions before we even know we will want to pose them.

Journalism and fiction went hand in hand for Roth. Even as he experienced growing success with his fiction he kept writing newspaper articles. In a 1934 letter to a friend Roth insisted that *The Antichrist* was a Christian work and not a journalistic work, but the convenient device Roth utilized to send his protagonist around the world happens to be his employment by a newspaper editor. The malevolence of the book's 'Master of a Thousand Tongues' is likely a mirror of Roth's feelings about the power wielded by Fascist and Communist newspaper editors. Perhaps Roth's refusal to call *The Antichrist* a journalistic work was his acknowledgement that it was not objective but subjective. While it was written with journalistic sensibilities, it presents the blunt philosophical observations and pointed accusations of an essayist, wrapped together with a loose fictional plot.

In *The Antichrist* the multiple and often contradictory realities of modern life are presented primarily through the use of dialogue. The more subtle use of targeted descriptive passages was more or less discarded (with a few exceptions); instead, Roth employed his reporter's knack for asking the right questions and then switching viewpoints to answer them. In fact, some sections of dialogue read rather like interviews or political debates.

The protagonist of *The Antichrist* editorializes freely through the use of these dialogues with an army of characters representing opposing (and quite often malignant) points of view. These characters, either blindly ignorant or outright malevolent, argue with Roth's standpoint and counter his propositions with their own views of the world. In some ways Roth found within the open structure of *The Antichrist* a means to tackle within a few pages the types of issues that took the entire length of one of his conventional novels.

Roth also served up equal parts of irony and cynicism to help dispatch various subjects more quickly. The multiple realities of Roth's world were quite conducive to irony, and *The Antichrist* is filled with a cynical yet lyrical irony when confronting the modern condition. When the hero of *The Antichrist* joins the army during the Great War he describes the events one morning thus: 'We had halted, that is to say, in the parlance of war, that we could rest before beginning once again to shoot and to die.'

At times in Roth's work his irony amounts to a simple literary nod or a sarcastic wink; at others it is a grand and eloquent undercurrent that swells until the plot reaches a crescendo. For literary works to evoke such strong irony implies that the author has developed an excellent sense of perspective. In part through his keen powers of observation and in part to his well-developed overview on

European history, much of Roth's work is highly prescient. It is no coincidence that it was Roth who was the first European writer to mention Adolf Hitler in a work of fiction, all the way back in 1923. Another example of his startling ability to foresee the future is the pre-Holocaust *The Wandering Jews*, a surprising read today not only because it captures the mid-1930s tension and uncertainty of European Jewish life so perfectly but because it loudly signals the cataclysmic events to come.

The Antichrist, too, is amazingly visionary because it both predicts and laments the course of the rest of the twentieth century. Fortunately for us as readers of Joseph Roth, his writing career spanned one of the most interesting and turbulent times in modern history, including the First World War and the end of the Austro-Hungarian monarchy, the end of Imperial Russia, the Russian Revolution and Communism, the Weimar Republic and the rise of Fascism and Hitler. The litany of problems that Roth cites within the book – racism, unchecked capitalism, socialism, religious persecution, revolution and social upheaval – would plague the world of the late 1930s and far beyond. What might have seemed a bit paranoid to some readers of the day comes across today as amazingly insightful. How else to describe a chapter called 'The Iron God', in which a Nazi, in conversation with the protagonist, described how it is through the swastika that they will conquer the world, not only vanquishing other peoples but also their gods.

The thematic thread through Roth's fiction is generally nostalgia for the 'old days'. Although his fatherless youth may not have been idyllic, Roth experienced and enjoyed life in a pre-war frontier-town Galicia, an existence he would describe in many of his books, notably *Weights and Measures*. His benevolence towards the Austro-Hungarian monarchy stemmed from a deep-seated belief that what came after was far crueller and much more unstable than the autocratic empire-building of the Habsburgs. The same might be said of his feelings towards Imperial Russia (Roth's brief romance with Communism ended after he visited the Soviet Union). Roth's post-war world, as seen in *Hotel Savoy*, *Rebellion* and several other novels of his, is one of chaos, social unrest and cynicism. In these books Roth presented the aftermath of the First World War through the lens of one or more characters who are decidedly *pre*-war in their philosophy. In *The Antichrist*, however, nostalgia for the past is brushed aside and replaced by alarm at the course the present was taking towards the future. If Roth's other books detail the agonizing transition from the old ways of Europe to the new world that existed after 1918, *The Antichrist* looks past the transition to focus on the stark realities of the modern world.

Sadly, in *The Antichrist* Joseph Roth is also foreshadowing his own premature demise, explaining and lamenting his growing inability to fit into the new world that was rapidly taking shape around him. Part of his profound melancholy during the middle and later 1930s was a product of what he viewed to be the gullibility of many people and, further, their powerlessness in the face of evil. His rather blunt assessment in *The Antichrist* that everyone contains the seeds of hatred for the Jews sprang equally from his awareness that a very dark hour had come for European Jews and from his understanding that people could easily be swayed more easily to hate than to love. Similarly, his admonition that people were given feet so that they might leave a country where injustice is done to them was a warning for German Jews to follow his lead and leave before it was too late.

Roth's malaise only increased over time as the influence of Fascism and Communism threatened to take over the world. He was clearly disturbed by the German concordat with the Catholic Church in 1933, and this event forms the basis of the concluding chapter of *The Antichrist*. The exiled Roth's *Angst* over the state of the world continued to increase after that and reached a crescendo in 1938 with the German annexation of Austria, after which he told a friend sadly: 'I have lost my country. I have nothing left.'

Roth's growing unease about the world around him is reflected in *The Antichrist*; even as he wrote it the situation deteriorated. The confident protagonist of the beginning of book, who says he is not afraid of the Antichrist, later gives way to a wary protagonist who admits he *is* afraid. Fortunately, while a sense of despair haunts each page, it is tinged with the wry humour of one who has the upper hand. One gets the sense that in unmasking the Antichrist at every turn Roth prevails. He saw the truth and was spreading the word, telling us to be wary of the trappings of our modern lives – of newspapers, of Communism, of corporations, of religion or atheism, of racist thoughts. He was clearly outraged at the trickery and inequality of the modern world – not so much at the technological wonders themselves as at their shameless uses for manipulation and deception. Exposing the Antichrist in his various guises was Roth's best weapon against him. In revealing the evils lurking among us Roth hoped to prompt people, corporations and nations towards ruthless self-examination and propel them to action, evicting the Antichrist from their presence.

Some of Roth's perceived evils are more obviously insidious than others. One of the more controversial and perhaps bizarre stances throughout the book is that taken against Hollywood and the film industry, especially in the chapter titled 'Hollywood, the Hades of Modern Man'. Wary of our dependence on the technological advances of the early twentieth century, Roth realized their immense power to control people. At the start of the chapter he writes how 'the false heart of a false friend' thousands of miles away can only be magnified over the telephone. Here Roth correctly predicted the influence of radio, microphones and loudspeakers (and later television) as propaganda, foreseeing their growing use by Hitler, Goebbels and Mussolini as tools to control the masses. One can only imagine what Roth might say about the dangers of today's technology – email, text messages, mobile phones and the internet. What seems bizarre at first becomes less outrageous as one realizes the scope of Roth's prescience.

As regards actors and the public fascination with them, Roth was again spot on with observations that seem especially true in today's celebrity-crazed culture of paparazzi stalkers and tabloid newspapers paying millions for photographs of celebrity babies. In describing how the actor sells out and provides his shadow on screen for all eternity Roth wrote: 'Yes, one could say that he is even less than a shadow of himself, since the shadow is actually his true existence.' Yet Roth's true feelings about the cinema may not have been so harsh; the same year the first English translation of *The Antichrist* was published Twentieth Century Fox was busy making a film based on his novel *Job*.

The Antichrist was not only a product of its turbulent times but also the turbulence of Roth's own personal situation. After his reluctant flight from Germany in 1933, what had already been a life of questionable happiness and stability took a drastic turn into a downwards spiral from which escape would be impossible. While *Job* sold about 30,000 copies and *Radetzkymarch* sold a very respectable 40,000 copies in Germany, after Hitler took power Roth's future in Germany was over. The blunt force of *The Antichrist's* arguments demonstrate a raw and emotional side of Roth that was usually not evident in his books, as if he was releasing some of the tension and anger that had accompanied his involuntary relocation. Roth never did find a permanent home during his exile, living out of hotel rooms in Paris and the many places he visited.

Between 1933, when he wrote the book, and 1935, by which time *The Antichrist* had been published first in German and then in English and other languages, Joseph Roth had a great many concerns weighing on his mind. Besides the rapidly crumbling stability of his beloved Europe he had an array of personal worries. He fretted constantly about his precarious financial situation, when he would be paid and how much he was owed. Although several of his books met with substantial critical and commercial success, he was nevertheless in need of funds. He complained that the Nazis had taken 30,000 marks of his money after he left in 1933. Whatever level of comfort and success he had achieved during the German years, by 1934 Roth was desperate for cash. At one point during his exile Roth sent money to his French translator for safekeeping for fear he himself could not be trusted with it.

While in exile Roth worked hard to keep track of the various foreign rights that had been sold and the translations of his works that were under way, a formidable task in itself. He also worried about the legal status of the children of his girlfriend, Andrea Manga Bell, a half-Cuban half-German woman whose husband had abandoned her.

During this time Roth often complained to friends about the poor state of his health. He sometimes signed his letters 'old Joseph Roth' and wrote frequently of being drained after working exhausting ten- or twelve-hour days on his various projects. These long days of work were his 'Waterloo', as he explained. He was often physically and mentally spent after writing, yet he hardly took a break, continuing to churn out new books one after another. He described himself in one letter as depressed, with 'mountains of chagrin', and in another letter said: 'I work in a great anguish, a true panic.'

Although only forty years old when *The Antichrist* was published,

Roth was by this time a physically ruined man. Excessive amounts of alcohol, chronic worry, overwork and a generally weak constitution had irreparably taken their toll. By the time of his death in May 1939 Roth had lived to see the world enveloped in a growing darkness that he had warned against six years earlier when writing *The Antichrist*. The last line of his book rings all too true. For just as his protagonist of the same name did, when Joseph Roth had seen enough he 'left the theatre', so to speak.

Although his pen was stilled so many decades ago, at long last Roth's warning to the world can finally be read again in English.

TRANSLATOR'S NOTE AND ACKNOWLEDGEMENTS

Joseph Roth said in a 1934 interview: 'For me, a good translation is that which renders the rhythm of my language.' I hope that I have met his standards, which, because of the differences in German and English syntax, can be a challenge. As I worked I tried to be as faithful to the spirit of the German original as possible. I carefully compared the original English translation of 1935 with Roth's German text of 1934 while creating the new translation of 2010. I have preferred to retain Roth's sometimes brief and emphatic sentences rather than combine them. For the most part I use the same paragraph breaks as Roth, rather than split longer paragraphs and combine shorter ones (the first English translation featured much of the latter). I have also tried not to eliminate any sentences in their entirety, even if repetitive. Precisely because Roth's emphatic writing style is a bit different in *Der Antichrist* than in his other books, I wanted to retain and highlight that difference. I have sought to preserve the tone and style of the original German version; the result is an interesting sermon-like quality in parts of the book, which I believe Roth fully intended. Fresh from being forced into exile from the country he loved, Roth was both angry and frightened, eager to warn the world of its dire situation, and I wanted to ensure that this came across in translation.

The original English translation glossed over some important moments in the book. One notable instance occurs on pages 94,

96 and 163, when in the original German Roth says 'Hollywood, ein Holle-Wut'. This play on words meaning 'hell fury' was entirely left out of the original English translation, probably because the translator simply did not know what to do with it. This wordplay in particular was a concern of Roth's at the time. In fact, he enquired of his French translator what she had done about it in her version. In this new English translation I have chosen to use 'Unholywood' as it sounds and looks close to Hollywood and has a meaning I believe is close enough to what Roth intended with his clever play of words. Using 'hell fury' in English would not make sense in the context; however, I do use it later in conjunction with a repeated use of 'Unholywood'. (Similar wordplay by Roth, the use of Edisons versus Edi-sohns, worked in English because *sohn* translates as 'son'.)

In dealing with the Hollywood film studio mentioned in the last chapter, I have gone with what the German original text says: 'Goldwein-Mutro-Meyer' (which is referred to twice and then, bizarrely, is switched to Mutro-Goldwein-Meyer), whereas the first English translation takes a less provocative path with 'Cinema Ltd'.

Interestingly, Roth used one English word in the entire book – 'nothing' – the word used by the Hollywood talent agents to tell the shadows there is no work to be had.

I would like to thank the wonderful Peter Owen, Antonia Owen and Simon Smith for their belief in this important project. I would also like to thank Simon Hamlet for his encouragement. Thanks also to the Leo Baeck Institute in New York.

Richard Panchyk
New York, 2010

THE ANTICHRIST

I have written this book as a warning
and exhortation, that one might recognize
the Antichrist in all the forms in which he appears.

THE ANTICHRIST HAS COME

How lonesome it is in such times with he who clings only to the intellectual! Ah, for whom should one write, in the midst of political clamour and shouting that deafen the ears to more moderate sounds . . . with whom one can enter into a theological debate, since theology has fallen into the hands of doctrinaires and zealots, whose last and best argument for their point of view is to horse-riding troops and cannon? Your hunt . . . has begun: with ball and chain and hangman's sword you think you serve the cause of Christianity . . . Rome, the glory of the world, has been conquered by mercenaries – oh God, what bestial instincts rage in your name! No, the world no longer has room for the freedom of the heart! . . . And now you die, Erasmus! – Stefan Zweig, *Erasmus of Rotterdam*

The Antichrist has come; so disguised that we, who have been expecting him for years, cannot recognize him. Already he lives in our midst, among us. And over us spreads the heavy shadow of his vile wings. We are already smouldering in the icy glow of his hellish eyes. Our unsuspecting throats near the reach of his strangling hands. Already is he licking at our world with the blasphemous flames of his tongue. Already is he lifting his fiery feet so he can stomp on the flimsy and flammable roofs of our homes. Long has he been pouring poison into the innocent souls of our children. But we do not notice!

For we have been struck with blindness, with the blindness that it is written will befall us at the end of time. In fact, for a long time now we have not been able to recognize the nature and face of things that we encounter. Just like the physically blind, we have only names for all these things in the world that we can no longer see. Names! Names! Sounds without shape. Hollow tones with which to clothe unimaginable and therefore bodiless and lifeless phenomena. Are they shapes? Are they shadows? The blind cannot differentiate one from the other. We, the blind, recognize nothing. To real things we give false names. Hollow words ring in our poor heads, and we no longer understand the meaning of the words. We can no longer recognize form, colours or dimensions. We only have names and terms for form, colours and dimensions. Since we became blind, we apply these names and terms incorrectly. We call something big small, something small big, the black white and the white black; shadows light and light shadows; the bright dull and the dull bright. Thus names and terms are devoid of content and meaning. It is worse than at the time of the Tower of Babel. Then, only tongues were confused and one man could not understand another, for each had different names for the same things. Now we all speak the same but false language, and all things have the same but false terms. It is as if we are building a horizontal Tower of Babel, but the blind, who are unable to recognize dimensions, believe it is vertical and growing ever higher; and they believe that everything is in order because they understand each other perfectly . . . whereas their comprehension of the proportion, form and colour of things is only that of the blind. That is to say, they apply terms that were originally applied correctly, and which fit the phenomena of this world, in a false and inverted sense; the towering is flat and the flat towering. For a blind man cannot distinguish between what is high and what is low. At the time of the Tower of Babel it was only people's tongues and ears that were confused. A few of the builders could still understand each other by the language of the eyes, the mirrors of the soul, as they say. But now, people's eyes are blinded (and tongues are just servants, while eyes are masters in the hierarchy of the human senses). How can people still hope that the Antichrist has not yet come? This faith and this hope are further evidence of our blindness. For just as one can convince a blind man that night is day and day is night, so can we, who have been blinded, make ourselves believe that the Antichrist is not in the world, that we are not burning in the fire of his eyes, that we are not standing in the shadow of his wings.

But our blindness is worse than mere physical blindness of the type I have already described. For our blindness is one that can only be struck by the Antichrist, and that, as I said at the beginning, will be our doom before the end of time. It is a hellish blindness, for although we were blinded we think we can see. In truth, we are 'blinded' rather than 'blind'. We do not recognize the Antichrist because he comes dressed as an average citizen, in the garb of a commoner in every land. According to the legendary image we have of him, he should have come with all the hellish accessories, with his traditional attributes: horn, tail and cloven hoof, stinking of pitch and sulphur, enveloped by all the theatrical traits our childish fantasies demand from a creature of his nature and origins. People do not like to think that someone who looks just like them can bring them to ruin. Our egotism requires certain formalities at the hour of our ultimate death. But the Antichrist tries to outsmart us. He comes in the everyday dress of a commoner, yes, equipped even with all the signs of the base piety of the middle class, his innocent-seeming greed and what he imagines to be sublime love for certain human ideals – for example, faithfulness until death, love for the fatherland, heroic readiness to sacrifice himself for the whole, chastity and virtue, reverence for the tradition of his fathers and of the past, dependence on the future and respect for the high-sounding parade of phrases with which the average European is accustomed, even bound, to live. In this innocent-seeming masquerade has the Antichrist recently arrived into the world. For centuries we had been expecting his appearance in a spectacular theatrical entrance. Now that he has come, however, not as a destroyer stinking of sulphur but sometimes even as a pious man cloaked in incense, crossing himself while greeting us, murmuring the Lord's Prayer as he plays the stock exchange, praising human virtue (lowered to 'bourgeois' virtue) so he can destroy us, pretending to defend European culture with the very weapons with which he destroys it, promising to honour the past and proclaiming a future (all the while knowing that after him there will be none), promising to redeem mankind and humanity while he brings men to their deaths, as though his lying tongue does not know what acts his murderous hand is committing. Now that he has come in such a deceitful guise we have not recognized him, the Antichrist.

But I have uncovered him. I see through him when, in the east of this failing continent he proclaims the freedom of the workers and the ennoblement of work; when in the West he promises to defend the freedom of culture and raises the false flags of humanity over the roofs of prisons; when in Central Europe (meaning between east and west) he promises a nation blessings and prosperity while laying the groundwork for the war that will destroy it; when he persuades the island race of Europe, the English, the sailors of the old continent, to maintain indifference to all that may occur on the mainland – as seafaring sailors, although sons of the mainland, can be persuaded to disregard the fate of the homes in which they were born; when he promises the sons of the European mountains, the Swiss, and the children of the coast, the Dutch, profit and fortune from the mutual destruction of others; when he pits the yellow races against the white and the blacks against both; when he offers the Italians the might of Ancient Rome and the Greeks the glory of Ancient Hellas. Yes, even when he, the Prince of Darkness, visits the Vatican and dictates concordats . . . I recognize him, the Antichrist.

And although his power is far greater than mine, I fear him not – and will try to unmask him.

A FORCE HAS COME BETWEEN US
AND THE GRACE OF REASON

This has also been attempted, in order to guard against surprise;
surprise is imitated, they try to anticipate it using machines.
They manufacture technical surprises, so that it may seem as
though there were only these and that spiritual ones were no
longer possible. Surprise has been mechanized. There exists
today a machinery of surprise. In the technical, there is such a
tremendous potential today, that everything seems possible. All
possibilities are contained in this machinery, and they need no
longer become reality. And thus whatever becomes reality can
never surprise – one knows that everything was already inherent
in the great machines. – Max Picard, *The Human Face*

I have already said that the Antichrist did not come with pitch and
sulphur as we had imagined he would arrive. His entrance was so
excellently prepared that the hellish elements had long before
been transformed into those that were seemingly natural, familiar
and earthly. I should not be understood as agreeing with the opinion
of those narrow-minded advocates of the view that industry and
technical civilization are the works of hell. No! I am far removed
from this viewpoint. For I believe that God himself has bestowed
upon us the reason to investigate, to enquire, to uncover answers
and solutions, better answers and solutions and still better
answers and solutions. We were granted intelligence so that with its

help we might relieve our hands of their heavy burden and gradually learn to hold high our heads, which were made in the image of God, so that they may project towards the heavens where, as it were, their sublime and eternal reflection is mirrored. When man was exiled from paradise and condemned to cultivate the earth in the sweat of his brow, limitlessly mild God – for He blesses even where he punishes – gave him the grace of reason to lighten his way, a memory of paradise, so to speak, a shining memory, a tiny jewel from the endless crown of divine wisdom. The good God gave man the blessing of reason to make the curse of labour milder and lighter. They are thus fools and knaves who say that inventions and discoveries are a curse, that machines are vices. But it is a vice to characterize invention, discovery, the fruits of research and the perceptions of the mind as victories that human understanding has gained over the eternally secret wisdom of the Infinite. As a tiny pebble to a mighty boulder, so does our ability to discover and invent compare with the wisdom of the Power that rules over us. For we have, as an example, conquered the air (for the moment), but this does not allow us to fly up to Heaven. Not only has it been ordained, as the proverb goes, that trees cannot reach Heaven, neither can men visit it. And never will we see a pilot harness the power that resides in an angel's wings. Yes, one could say that Heaven becomes ever higher and ever further away from earth the higher and further we fly. And when we have reached the so-called stratosphere we have done nothing other than transport our earthly selves to a sphere that so far no earthly inhabitant has reached. We have lifted the earth upwards, so to speak; however, in no way have we brought Heaven downwards. And if we were able to climb even higher, to some unnamed planet, Heaven would recede even further away. (Let us take all this as a parable. Let us say that it is the nature of God's fathomless wisdom that it remains unfathomable.) Oh, we have no idea what is above and what is below! We are so blind! And although we point upwards in 'blind faith' as we refer to God, there may be no such thing as above. And the folly of those who believe they have discovered the emptiness of Heaven because during their flight into the stratosphere they searched but found no God would be a hundred times greater than is the blindness of those believers who point upwards when they name the origin and the source of their faith. What is 'above'? What is 'below'? Alas, the world is populated with nothing but blind people! These blind are also confused! Many of them say that they are wise because they found knowledge in a place that other blind men, with no thirst for knowledge, showed them. And since a segment of those without sight declared that God is 'above', another portion of the blind make their way 'above' and, having not seen God, come back and say that He is not there. The reason that they do not see Him, however, is that they are blind. If they could see there wouldn't be any need for them to make their way along the path that their blind brothers have showed them! One cannot see God with one's physical eyes! One cannot smell God with one's physical nose! One cannot hear God with one's physical ears! One cannot feel God with one's physical hands! For He has, and by no means without reason, given us only five senses. Had He wished that we should know Him during the span of our earthly life He would have granted us not five but a thousand senses. But He has given us no more than five! Perhaps so that we may not be capable of knowing Him in our lifetime.

And now, arrogant as we are, many among us believe that we can deny Him because we are powerless to know Him. We therefore take revenge for His severity. If He withholds the grace of knowing him, we say that He doesn't exist.

Among us, the common blind, are those who are specially

blind, those to whom one cannot explain the difference between night and day.

How could we have so misused our reason? And how is it that this, a gift from God, as mentioned, the unique and last memory of Paradise Lost, has led us to folly and the vice of arrogant behaviour, to blasphemous and false views?

It was in no way foolish, reckless or arrogant to use our faculties of reason, as I have said earlier, but in the course of its application a power that we cannot perceive with the help of our five senses has forced itself between us and the grace of reason that is our heritage; and thus the blessing became a curse. When we believed that we were capable of thinking clearly and logically, we were already confused. And, truly, it was not with the type of confusion that occurred at the time of the Tower of Babel but, rather, a confusion *within* the clarity itself. This clarity was not the same as the false clarity of a wanderer in the desert who takes a *fata Morgana* as reality and heads towards it. No, it was such that reality itself became a *fata Morgana*! It did not dissolve into the air when we reached it. It was physical; it was tangible. It was not our tired senses that gave in to an illusion but our fresh and well rested senses. As we were being led astray we were not suffering from what might be considered sickness or exhaustion; rather, it appeared to us to be quite natural. Our reasoning was intact, our senses were alive and the goal lay very clearly in front of us. We even reached it. But it was, none the less, a trick. And thus we are like wanderers in the desert who are capable of catching up with the deceptive mirage that beckons them, of taking up residence in houses and castles that do not exist, of quenching their thirst from fake springs, of resting in the shade of palms that are not there and refreshing themselves with dates that are not really fruit. They then believe that their thirst has been quenched, but they are still thirsty; that their bellies are full, but they are still hungry; that they have shelter, but they have none. So it is. Our satiety is still hunger and thirst; our home is still homelessness; and what we call reality is still an illusion, for what we call knowledge is a hoax. We believe that we are drinking from plentiful springs, but they are parched wells that are themselves thirsty.

HOLLYWOOD, THE HADES OF MODERN MAN

> This could be recognized in the ancient faces. They were all distinguished from each other as symbols of the inexhaustibility and abundance of God, and they were at the same time all like one another because of the consciousness that all diversity is born from a single Creator. This eternal combination of similarity and difference, both through God, characterizes the ancient faces.
> – Max Picard, *The Human Face*

If I may take but a single example from the vast field of our progress: we are able to speak with each other across thousands of miles, but can we therefore understand one another? Are we speaking the truth to each other simply because we have placed a miracle between us, one that consists of making our voices heard across thousands of miles? And when a friend in Australia speaks to his friend in Colombia, as they say 'by wireless', does this 'technical wonder' eliminate malice, lies or treachery from their speech? Isn't it, in fact, easier to lie when the speakers are not face to face? And even if it should become possible for me to see my friend in Cairo while he sees my face in Paris, would we recognize each other more easily that way than when we are standing next to each other in the same room? Shouldn't it be more difficult to recognize each other? Can a telescope transform the inability of my eye to recognize into an ability to recognize? On the contrary – the telescope, even if it is perfect, merely strengthens the visual acuity of an eye, no matter if the eye sees falsely or correctly, but it cannot change a deceptive, lying eye into a genuine and true eye. And if the false heart of a false friend were to tell me of his affection from a million miles distant, through use of the most powerful loudspeakers, the so-called technical wonder would not have transformed the falseness of his heart into integrity but would only have magnified it. And if we have succeeded in making shadows move on the screen of the cinema as if they were living people and, further still, to speak and sing, their motions, words and songs are by no means honest and genuine; rather, these wonders of the screen signify that the reality that they so remarkably copy wasn't difficult to recreate for the very reason that it wasn't real. In fact, the real people, the living ones, had already become so shadowy that the screen shadows were bound to seem real.

When, now and then, I come upon an actor whom I recognize because I have seen him in a film in the theatre, it seems to me that because I have seen him on the screen I am not looking at him but at his shadow, although it is certain (and my intelligence tells me so) that he is the originator of the shadow that I know from the screen. Nevertheless, when I meet the living and breathing man he becomes for me a shadow of his own shadow. If it were plausible – that is to say, if it were truly possible to animate the shadows that we project on to the screen with technology's assistance – I should certainly see in the living actor something more than just himself, a living being. I should rather see a person who has the power to infuse his shadow with the very breath of life. It is thus a mysterious force that condemns a living person, God's creation, bestowed with the divine gift of being able to animate his shadow on the screen, to appear as his own shadow. Yes, one could say that he is even less than a shadow of himself, since the shadow is actually his true existence;

he is not himself but, as it were, his own *doppelgänger* – a *doppelgänger* that has no existence; he is, this actor, the *doppelgänger* of his own shadow, one that he projects on to the screen daily. A single time he had his own form captured on film. A single time, but for all eternity the most fleeting of all fleeting things of our earthly existence (namely a shadow) will last as a reality. To be one's own *doppelgänger* would in itself be a frightful event! But what can we say to the fact that the *doppelgängers* of their own shadows are among us – living people, walking, living, eating, drinking and loving?

And it gets still *more* terrible. For even a *doppelgänger* must die – one day both the original *and* his *doppelgänger* will die. And when an ordinary man dies his shadow also disappears. But the actor who plays in the cinema will live for ever on the screen, the only real milieu of his actual life. That is to say, his shadow or, more accurately, his true self (for he is only the *doppelgänger* of his shadow) is 'eternal'. That is also to say, certain men have lived not as men but as shadows and therefore cannot die. They cannot die because they have never lived. They are shadows. They have willingly, more or less voluntarily, become shadows. They have sold their shadows for money and said these were not shadows but *actually themselves*. And they sold not only their lives; they also sold their deaths. Hollywood paid them. In exchange they forfeited their hope of salvation. They were not only shadows for their entire lives; *they remained shadows after their deaths*. On the screen, for which they had lived when they were still alive, they still had the chance to be alive and remain that way for all eternity. Because during their lifetimes they saw their shadows as themselves and sold them as themselves, and under such circumstances death was not a phenomenon with which they concerned themselves – once they had signed a contract with Hollywood. Perhaps an ordinary man still counts on eternal salvation. But a man who lives by being a shadow while he is alive possesses, as it were, his *own* eternal salvation. He is convinced – and not without merit – that the screen, for which he has already lived as a physical phenomenon, guarantees him a comprehensible, rationally believable eternity even after he is dead. The inventor of film has offered people the prospect of an immortality that they can understand while they yet live. The ancient world knew of a Hades that was the residence of the dead, those who had crossed into the shadow world.

The world in which we now live knows a Hades of the living – it is the cinema. *Hollywood is the modern Hades.* There, shadows become immortal during one's lifetime.

Indeed, 'modern' people are distinguished from ancient people mainly by the fact that they have already introduced Hades, the realm of shadows, into the world. The Hades of modern man is Hollywood.

THUS INVENTION, A GIFT OF THE MIND,
BECAME AN ELEMENT OF THE ANTICHRIST

But it would be easy and foolish, as I have already clearly stated, to curse invention and the reason from which it is born. For the inventor has done nothing other than apply God's gift of sense. If, however, one makes use of a divine gift and it then acquires an evil purpose, the evil element must have injected itself between the moment of invention and that of its application in real life. And just as gold, for example, should have been a gift of nature, a blessing of the earth, but has become an element of the Devil so, too, invention, a gift of reason, has become an element of the Antichrist. For the Antichrist becomes most clearly recognizable by the fact that he transforms what is essentially noble into something lowly. It is truly the nature of his existence and activity to desecrate the holy, to degrade the sublime, to pervert the true and to scar the beautiful. Not satisfied with his reign over what is in essence vulgar – for this is admittedly also a component of the earthly world – he seeks to extend his dominion over the noble. However, it could never fall under his power if it remained noble, so he first transforms it into something evil. He is like a dictator whose own land is a desert and who, in order to vanquish his flourishing neighbours, first turns those thriving places into wastes so that they are like his own. If he did not make them like his own, they *could not* be subservient to him.

But he, the Antichrist, is therefore worse than such a tyrannical ruler because a dictator can be seen, heard, felt and hated, whereas the Antichrist has the power to transform a thriving country into waste land and, in doing so, to dupe us into believing that the waste land is flourishing. And, when he destroys, we think he is creating. When he gives us a stone we believe he has given us bread. The poison from his glass tastes like the elixir of life. We think that he himself, the Prince of Darkness, is a son of both Heaven and earth; so long as we live, this seems to us more than being the son of Heaven alone. He enters thusly; he speaks thusly: 'You were promised Heaven, but I give you the earth. You were supposed to believe in an unfathomable God, but I turn you yourselves into gods. You thought that Heaven was more than earth, but earth itself is really a heaven!'

And since it is in our innate nature to yearn eternally to become God – because we never forget our origins and are reflections that are always searching for their prototype – we are seduced by the Antichrist. He can easily transform our most noble longings into lowly envy. For longing and jealousy are twin sisters, the one beautiful and the other ugly, who can nevertheless be mistaken for one another. It is inherent in our nature to want to be gods. The Antichrist, however, tells us we are already gods. And, as it is inherent in our imperfect nature that we grow tired and permit our senses to be tricked, he exploits our weaknesses and changes the milestones on our long path into goals. And we believe him. We are always searching, as long as we live, for our eternal home. But long before we have reached it we think that we are already there, thanks to the tricks of the Antichrist. And because our feet become weary, we believe him. Our home is still infinitely far away. But by no means do we go towards it. We halt by the wayside. We remain in the desert and imagine that we have reached our eternal home.

When a poor man tires of his poverty, how soon he stops fighting it and begins to see it as wealth! A prisoner who is serving out

a life sentence in gaol believes after ten years of solitary confinement that the prison yard is actually freedom. And thus we, who can
separate our shadows from our bodies so they act independently, as
though they were human, believe that we already possess the
divine power to bring something to life that does not exist.

What an illusion! We have, in fact, brought nothing to life!
We have instead granted the greater part of the short life that was
gifted us to our shadows! We have not created life; we have lost
it! We have not created; we have squandered! And we have
squandered sinfully.

THIS IS THE AIM OF THE ANTICHRIST:
TO DESECRATE ONE WONDER
THROUGH ANOTHER

It is not possible to talk about the Antichrist if one has not met him; and by this I mean if one has not met him actually and in the flesh. As for me, I have met him in many forms. Since my early youth our paths have crossed. I spoke before in such detail about the theatre of shadows because it was there that I first encountered him.

My first contact with the Antichrist happened many years ago, when I was still a boy and saw the wonder of the living shadow for the first time. There came a large vehicle, powered by unseen forces, which stopped at an open plaza outside of town and sent forth a large machine that was covered with a small canvas tent. Then a large tent, also of canvas, was pitched, spread and domed, and one could see upon entry that the interior of the dome was a blue sky with numerous gold and silver stars scattered about. And it was as real as the firmament. The human eye is not capable of seeing more of the actual heavens than can be shown on the spacious dome of a marquee, and the spectators' eyes therefore saw just as much or as little as they can see of the heavens when they look up at night. Blue was the dome, and the stars were just as unreachable and just as distant as real stars. Since we are not tall enough even to reach the roof of a circus tent erected by men, it was all the same to the people who sat under this roof if the sky was real or a reproduction. Neither one of them was within reach of their hands.

Consequently, they were quite willing to believe that the fake was real. And as it was very dark below and within this canvas tent the people inside believed that they were sitting under a bright and starry summer-night's sky. We heard an unfamiliar rattling and a humming and buzzing and chattering and thundering from some strange origin. And above and below we saw some kind of four-sided cone that was born from a minuscule square hole, the brightness of which was enveloped by black walls. This cone grew slowly and symmetrically over the spectators' heads, ever fuller, ever clearer, with its edges becoming more clearly visible in the pale light until it reached and filled the screen, as though a river of pale light were to pour itself into a sea of pallor, illuminating the latter through its own brightened pallor, so that it became visible as a four-sided sea. And we could see the vertical and horizontal threads stretched out on the four-sided sea. The four-sided cone that whirred above our heads made an incredible noise, and when we looked at it we were led to believe that the ruckus came from the billions of dust particles within rubbing against one another. Our ears were shocked that such minuscule molecules of dust and nothingness, even though there were billions of them, might be able to emit such an audible whir. So that we could no longer hear the sound of the dust molecules, an orchestra below the screen began to play marches and waltzes. And this, indeed, drowned out the whir of the dust molecules.

When the first shadows came to life on the rectangular screen and the marches and waltzes played up from the orchestra, the drums beating and the cymbals clashing, we could no longer hear the whirring of the dust particles. But we felt that the little square hole above our heads at the back of the crowd, the birthplace of the dust-laden cone, was the place where the life-sized shadows acquired their lives. Clearly, they sprang from the tiny four-sided hole and could remain unseen throughout their travels along the swelling cone until they made themselves visible on the screen in their deceptively large size. Yet they were shadows! They were less than the molecules of dust whose tiny bodies whirred so loudly in the cone of light. These shadows travelled unnoticed within the billions of dust particles, from the tiny, four-sided hole in the apparatus behind our backs to the four-sided sea that took form before our eyes.

There I saw naked women for the first time, that is to say, the shadows of naked women.

It is not my intention to suggest that this is a means of temptation used by the Antichrist.

For it was God who created naked people and not the Antichrist. And as we do not inherently see sin in nakedness, thus does the Antichrist want to seduce us by nakedness alone. No, not through nakedness does he reveal and betray himself but, rather, through the purpose for which he uses our nakedness and also our clothing.

On the screen they showed an Egyptian princess. She was bathing naked in the Nile with some naked playmates. She fished out a little box, daubed with pitch inside and out. In this box lay Moses, the future leader of the Jews, the lawgiver of the world.

Very small, infinitesimally small, was the box in which lay Moses, the leader of the Jews and lawgiver of the world.

But large and pretty were the breasts and thighs of the princess and her bathing friends, and, although the lawgiver of the world amounts to much more than a woman's breast, the box in which he lay immediately disappeared as though swallowed up by the cone of light, and the princess splashed towards the shore, and we saw her back as before we had seen her breasts.

And as everything in the world has its rank and degree, I believe that even the truth of true things is falsified and turned upside down when these are used as pretexts for that which is great and sub-

49

lime. So in using the wondrous discovery of mankind's lawgiver as an excuse for showing the beautiful back and pretty breasts of the Egyptian princess, they destroyed the beauty of her body.

And this is one of the aims of the Antichrist. It is ever his goal to desecrate *one* marvel through use of another. By this, too, we may recognize him.

Later the war was shown. It was the Russo-Japanese War. Entire regiments were marching. They didn't move from right to left or vice versa; rather, they came, as small as specks of dust at first from the background of the screen (which was not really a background), growing ever larger, swelling and marching directly towards us as they became ever more enormous, and they appeared as if they were about to trample over the front rows of spectators with their hob-nailed boots. The first double row of marching soldiers were already lifting their massive feet to step upon our necks, and we began to duck in anticipation of the footfalls. But then they vanished, just as shadows vanish. They couldn't survive outside of the screen. They had achieved as much as shadows can achieve. They had been able to grow, to swell to the size of a colossus. But in the same degree to which they grew larger they also became more transient and empty, and the textured surface of the screen began to show under the impending threat of their iron-shod boots. They were large, these shadows, but also porous. Holes appeared, bright holes, in the midst of their vast bodies, and the more threatening they seemed the more powerless they grew. The first column dissolved into space, then the second, the third, the fourth, the tenth. Soon we realized that we didn't need to duck any more. But, just as this terror was overcome, an even greater one attacked us. And this was caused by our realization that the columns marching towards us were the images of actual troops. In the instant they were filmed marching they had been alive. Through the act of filming they had become shadows, the shadows they should not have become until later but which they actually became shortly after the film had been shot. We were seized with terror at the sight of them, because we were not yet accustomed, as are people today, to seeing living shadows without living bodies, and so at that moment we did not know if the shadows that were marching towards us were actually those of fallen soldiers. In one or another of the spectators this might have awakened the memory of the biblical scenes they had just viewed, that is, the breasts of the bathing Egyptian girls. And since the latter, as every child had to know, were dead and decaying for thousands of years, this understanding helped confirm that the shadows were those of dead soldiers.

So the true wonder, which uplifts us or flushes us with a fervent bliss, is different from the so-called technological wonder, which merely terrifies or amazes us or fills us with arrogance about the progress we have achieved. For we know that the latter was achieved through 'natural things'. So we quickly recover from our fear and astonishment (while our arrogance increases), and we think about it and come to the conclusion that the bathing Egyptians are our living contemporaries who have set aside their clothing and sold the shadows of their naked bodies for money; shadows that were paid for just as real bodies are paid for in this world. But if this was the case with the girls, how was it with the soldiers? Surely they had not sold their shadows for money. And what an injustice, what a special injustice, even compared with the injustices that we have become used to in this world and which we have gradually come to perceive as right. The girls had been given money merely for doing healthful and pleasant work – for bathing in a river. On the other hand, the soldiers, who were marching to their deaths and were about to become true shadows, had not been paid a penny for giving up their shadows. Yes, at the moment they were off to meet their suffering, in the last hour of their lives, their shadows had been stolen at a moment when they could not think of asking for money. We, however, were paying for them with our entry fee, in other words, in order to see them heading to their deaths (just as we had paid to see naked, bathing Egyptians). And because the soldiers had not requested payment for their shadows, it was really *they* who were paying for the shadows of the bathing girls! Even if the film producer was committing a base fraud by pretending to show the discovery of Moses when in reality he only showed a tiny box (but life-sized shadows of women), yet at least he had invested money in *this* sham – money that even the law says justifies this or that. But the soldiers who were going to their deaths had received no payment from the man. He had stolen their shadows. And even in our world, in which money plays a role in justice, theft is punished. However, the man who animated the cinema with shadows could not be punished since otherwise it would not be possible to charge an entrance fee to exhibit the product of his crime. If only he had stolen the shadows of soldiers heading towards their deaths to demonstrate how many men must die for a cause that has no concern with any individual among them – but, no, he had actually stolen their shadows for the very same reason that he had bought those of the naked girls. For he knew that we were human, and he offered to us both the lust of the flesh and the horrors of death. He was deliberately playing on our sensuality, directed equally towards the flesh of our living brothers and living sisters as towards the horrible destruction of our neighbour. He exploited our human frailty, through theft if possible, and when he could not steal, through money. And so he put on a so-called 'programme' such as is still shown in all the cinemas of the world today.

To whom can it be due that a fruit of human reason, and therefore of divine grace, has been utilized, from the very first instant of its practical application, to distort that reason?

Which of all the forces that control our existence is equipped with such malice and power that it can pay bathing girls and steal from dying men? Is he just an ordinary thief? Is he not more likely the same one who pays young girls to undress and enter the water while he arms men and sends them to their deaths, selling the shadows of the one and the other for the price of a ticket? Had he really robbed the soldiers of their shadows? Is he not far more mighty than just a thief or robber? Who can use the miraculous rescue of the lawgiver of the world as an excuse for girls to undress? Who can thus play upon our sensuality, which craves living flesh with the same intensity with which it devours horrible death? Who can thus transform the gift of reason into a curse? Who has the power to pay girls who are merely bathing and to rob the dying soldiers? And both at the same time? Had he not arranged a war between Russia and Japan? Just as easily as he arranged a bath for the naked girls? Did he not select the very moment when our reason began to do wondrous things to fool us? The very moment at which we believed that we could not be blinded, since we were performing so-called miracles? Can one fool gods? And do we not think that we are gods because we are in the process of learning from the gods how to perform miracles and even to make them intelligible? This is the moment for the Antichrist, this moment in which we take ourselves for gods because we perform miracles that we understand, even though we are not gods.

This is his hour; this is the hour of the Antichrist.

AND I ALSO BECAME A SOLDIER

Then there came unto the world the Great War, which is called the World War; many became soldiers, and I also became a soldier.

We know that all around the world the Antichrist mingles with the soldiers as he has always done; with soldiers, who are compelled to regard life lightly while continually in the presence of Death, for it is actually Death who is their father and not the kaiser, and the 'other world' is their real fatherland even during their lifetime. It is therefore remarkable that the sons of Death should also let themselves be seduced by earthly things, that they should live for earthly glory and conceive a love for it. Although the Evil One can rarely seduce them with the clinking coins that others put into their wallets, he seduces soldiers with similar, somewhat larger coins which they can pin on to their chests. And he also seduces them through stars and buttons, through stripes and braids. I have seen so many who, one hour before we marched forth to sink into the arms of our father, Death, hastily obtain through cunning, baseness, the shabby trick of foolish ambition or even by physical violence, one more star, one more button, one more length of braid, so that he might be distinguished by these things from the others at the very second that they are all about to die. The train that carried us to the battlefield contained different kinds of cars, and in the better ones were those who had more braid and better buttons.

The first thing I will relate is that during the time when we were training and learning to use weapons we had various mundane tasks to perform on a daily basis. So one day I went out with a squad of soldiers whose job it was to collect metal throughout the town from which would be made cannon and cannonballs – latches, candlesticks and, in general, all kinds of domestic utensils that contained copper, brass, nickel, iron or steel. A large wagon covered with a canvas roof was driven into the courtyard of the barracks, and it was similar to the one that had delivered the first film theatre into our town. We were twenty-four soldiers, and the twenty-fifth, or, more accurately, the first, was the sergeant. When the horses were harnessed and the driver was ready to pull on the reins, the gate of the barracks was opened wide, and into the courtyard rolled a large black automobile with soft curtains spread over its windows. From the car stepped a very friendly black-clad gentleman carrying a black briefcase. Everything about him was dignified and kind – his pointed grey beard, his thick soft moustache and the gentle brown eyes with which he inspected us. From the pockets of his overcoat he withdrew chocolate bars and packs of cigarettes, and everyone received some of one and some of the other. If we had been one hundred or even one thousand, even then, none of us would have left empty-handed. This gentleman was like a kind yet powerful father. His mild, charitable hands had the ability, as soon as they were plunged into the depths of his pockets, to produce presents that he hadn't even brought with him. He smiled at us, got back in his car and drove on ahead of us. And where he stopped we also stopped, went into homes and retrieved domestic utensils to put in our large wagon. After we had emptied many houses the black car stopped before a church. Here the mild gentleman stepped out and hurried up the steps with his hat in his hand. We followed him and stood, our caps in our hands, in the golden twilight of the church.

The sexton came. The gentleman murmured something. The gentleman motioned to us, and we followed the sexton. We entered a small yard bordering the church. In the yard stood two bells, church bells, covered with verdigris as though with bluish-green velvet cloaks. They were old bells. Just as men attain the dignity of silver in old age, so do old bells acquire the dignity of verdigris, which is a kind of moss for metals, so that we are reminded of the ground in thick forests and of all types of ancient rocks and walls and stones. The bells were heavy. And as it was the first day we had been assigned to such a task we lacked suitable equipment, and while we were considering how we could lift the bells the kind gentleman came and said we should first overturn them and then roll them out of the yard. So we laid the bells down and saw that they were hollow bells, missing their clappers, which are the souls of bells; they were thus empty and dead bells. The gentleman bent down, and when he noticed that the clappers were missing he asked the sexton about it. So two of us went with the sexton and returned with the clappers. We then rolled away the bells with our hands, although it would have been easier to push them with our feet. But we didn't dare. The empty bells echoed dully against the stones of the yard. Next, we threaded thick ropes through the holes, tied one end of each rope to a side of the wagon, and by mounting the vehicle we were able to hoist the bells up. We then drove on with two dead church bells, one on each side of the wagon. We stopped again in front of a large red-brick building outside of town, and in a great hall that already contained thousands of metal utensils of the type that we had brought with us (and hundreds of bells both laying and upright) we unloaded the contents of our wagon, the booty of our labours. And the clappers were put into a large zinc kettle. As we dumped them they emitted a ringing sound, as though they had remembered that they were bell clappers that were supposed to ring.

The bells were made into cannon. Later I was sent to the front. And on the side of one of the many roads through which we passed stood a kind gentleman, still young in years, clad from head to foot in brown leather and wearing large goggles that were part of his leather helmet. Now there seemed to be something missing from this helmet. I didn't know what, but it was quite obvious that there was something missing. Only much later did I realize that what was missing from the helmet was horns. This leather-clad gentle-man gave us all chocolate and cigarettes, which he extracted from a roomy leather sack carried by two soldiers. He then hurried back to the side of the road, and we marched past him again (as is normally done only for generals and other high military officers) while he turned the crank on a black box that had a round glass eye in the middle. This eye swallowed all of our shadows. So now I knew that many years before the shadows of the Russian and Japanese soldiers had been bought with chocolate and cigarettes. And I could already envision our shadows on the screens of theatres throughout the land.

Shortly before Christmas a black automobile came and stopped just behind the battlefield where dead soldiers lay, and several gentle-men stepped out of the car. Among them was one who seemed especially kind and dignified. We all liked him immediately, mainly because of his reassuring grey beard. We had halted, that is to say, in the parlance of war, that we could rest before beginning once again to shoot and to die. We were marched not far from the black automobile. The kind-looking gentleman spoke to us. And what he said pleased us because of his gentle and agreeable voice.

He ordered a number of large leather sacks to be fetched, and it took twenty of us to lug these sacks, from which chocolate and cigarettes were distributed to the soldiers. At this time an aviator began to circle over our heads. And since the aviator was one of the enemy (called in the language of war 'an enemy pilot') he dropped a bomb. And then the black automobile vanished, smoke and stench rising from the place where it had stood. The kind gentleman turned around and left, accompanied by the others, who were somewhat more rigid-looking. Then a large grey car owned by the general pulled up and took away these gentlemen, whom we never saw again.

And when we returned to the battlefield, which in the language of war is known as 'the trenches', on the night that Jesus Christ was born, many of us died with pockets full of cigarettes and chocolate. These good gifts were taken by the survivors from the pockets of the fallen. And the guns made from bells continued to launch their thunder over our heads and towards those who, in the language of war, were known simply as 'the enemy'.

While we are speaking about the bells, I must explain how I was reminded of them after the war when I was poor and searching for work. There was employment to be had in the large red-brick building where we had once unloaded the metal and the bells, a place called the arsenal. We went there in search of work. In the great hall lay cannon, some whole, some damaged, some broken in pieces. There stood the gentle, grey-bearded man with the mild golden-brown eyes, and he directed us what to do. We loaded the broken weapons on to iron carts, and some of us smashed the undamaged ones with hammers. Outside, a large covered wagon was waiting. We loaded the cannon remnants on to it, and when it was so full that it could hold no more we drove it to a large factory, and there we unloaded the remains of cannon and guns.

The factory supervisor (who looked like our sergeant) made sure that everything was unloaded.

'What are you going to make with it?' I asked the supervisor.

'All kinds of useful things,' said the supervisor. 'The war is finished, my friend! We're going to make latches, locks, doors, candlesticks, mortars and bells – yes, church bells.'

THE CANNON AND THE BELLS

Since that time, whenever I hear the song of the bells, it seems as if gun barrels are swaying over the roofs and the towers of the churches, as if they are being swung not by worthy sextons or cheerful boys but by the one of whom I am speaking in this book. Has he not already so confused the ears of men that they find the thundering of cannon pleasant, even sweet, but the song of the bells unbearable? And has he not he apparently given these men the right to have perverted hearing and to be proud of it?

Ask the people in that expansive country where fools call themselves 'godless' before God has abandoned them (and only because they think they have abandoned Him) – ask them what the bells have done to them that they extract them from the churches.

They will give the following reply: 'The bells toll and boom and disturb our rest.'

And ask them whether the booming of the bells is more unmelodious than, for example, the howling of sirens or the discordant singing of crowds of people in the streets on various festive occasions or ten gramophones being played simultaneously in a single, thin-walled house.

They will reply: 'Sirens and gramophones have never been turned into cannon with which to kill us.'

And say further: 'Then mustn't you also banish the latches and metal vessels from your houses?'

They will then reply: 'The latches and vessels were taken from us more or less by force.'

'But,' you will then ask, 'wasn't violence also used upon the churches when their bells, their golden tongues, were removed?'

And the answer will be: 'As they began to shoot the cannon, the golden tongues also began to toll to announce that the hour of killing had arrived. And it is entirely correct to say that the bells themselves then began to kill, as they became cannon and guns. Since they have lied once, how can we believe that they now speak the truth? That is why the thunder of cannon, the false and inharmonious singing of the crowd, the bawling of apparatus, and the howling of sirens is more pleasing to our ears than the clanging of bells.'

So you enquire further: 'But don't the crowds and the gramophones and the sirens also lie – and don't the cannon lie and kill at the same time?'

And the people will answer: 'We don't believe that.' They will give this answer because people have faith in new things that they haven't yet caught in a lie; towards those things that they used to venerate, but which have deceived them, they are quite cruel.

It is easier for the Antichrist to scoff at the venerable and inexplicable by setting up man's reason as a judge and, in flattering it, flattering man himself. Nothing pleases a man so much. If he is told that he is handsome, strong, brave, affectionate, kind – he is delighted. Tell him he is clever – and he is blissful. And he will believe you merely because you have told him that he is clever, for he assumes that you would never try to lie to someone who is discerning.

I, however, who have always known that the Antichrist finds it easier to pollute the amazing products of our reason with his breath than the consecrated objects of our faith – even though he finds it easier to defame the latter – I am struck with horror at the broad scope of power that he already wields. If the sons of Edison, the Edi-sons, the sons of Edom, have fallen under his control, what does that matter? But he has swung himself on to the roofs of the churches and sits astride their spires; he takes the bells out of the belfries, and he renders the churches dumb; he rips the clappers from the bells and makes them empty – and have we not seen him with our own eyes leap with a single bound from the church spire where he had been sitting to the cross and bend it crooked, up and down and right and left, with the hateful strength of his arms and legs?

And this terrifies me more than his power over the products of our reason. For this is the first time he has had the profound insolence to bestow upon his name a visible and victorious symbol. Here, for the first time, he has emerged from the anonymity in which he had hidden himself. He has even had the audacity to print a calling card. And he announces himself in his true guise – namely as the Antichrist – *through the Anticross.*

THE MASTER OF A THOUSAND TONGUES

After we had taken all the pieces of guns that were formerly bells to the factories where they were to be turned into bells once again, we were all without employment, and each of us went in search of the kind of work to which he was best suited.

I went every morning to stand in front of one of the mightiest buildings, one in which newspapers are produced, those thousand-tongued messengers on the backs of which each day are printed enquiries both from men seeking work and employers seeking men under the title 'Employment Market'; that is to say, where work is offered for sale.

As I couldn't find any employment, my vanity led me to enter the great building and not to leave as did the others. In my foolishness, I thought that a building whose doors and walls were a market for work must likewise have work for sale within, and that the exterior alone of such a building would not reveal to me what it knew within its depths.

So I went to the master of this great house and asked him if he had any work for me.

At first glance I thought that I knew him. But I couldn't remember where I had seen him before. He was a gentle master, without a beard, and I thought that I had met him when he had worn a beard, but I couldn't recall the occasion.

He had a pleasant voice and a kindly glance. When he looked

at me I immediately believed that he wished me well, and as his face seemed so familiar to me I felt that he must have also been well acquainted with me.

When he asked whether I would be willing to serve him, I said: 'Yes, I will, with pleasure.'

Thus I began to serve him and so became one of the thousand tongues with which the newspapers meddle in the world every morning. I soon saw, however, that what my own tongue said was not only different from what the other tongues said but that all our thousand tongues were contradicting one another and that even this contradiction was no immutable law, as at one moment our tongues agreed, while at another they accused one another of lying, and this changed from moment to moment.

Many tongues repeated what mine had said but repeated it differently and in such a way that we were both wrong. I no longer knew if I had spoken truth or falsehood or whether the others were right or wrong, and when I realized that the world hears all our thousand tongues at the same time then I understood that it is entirely impossible for the world to recognize the voice of truth even if it should one day be heard.

But if I was one of the thousand confusing tongues that made the voice of truth unrecognizable then I was also guilty of confusing the world. And I realized that I had entered into the service of the Antichrist, who sat in this great publishing house as a gentle Master of a Thousand Tongues and smiled with kind eyes. And sometimes, so that his very gentleness might not betray him, he pretended to be furious. This, too, brought him profit, for when he let his anger subside and began to smile again, so that those who were under his command could once more exhale, their fears quieted, he appeared to them to be even more gentle, agreeable, good and honourable than before – and so they praised and esteemed him beyond measure, regarding themselves lucky that they came to be in his service and not in anyone else's.

When I grew to suspect that I was serving the Antichrist I decided one day to leave his employment. I went to him and told him that I'd had enough of his job and that he must likewise have had enough of my services.

He smiled and took from his pocket a gold cigarette case, asked me to take a seat and told me to have a smoke.

Then I remembered him – I did know him. How often he had already given me cigarettes!

And to make sure that I was not mistaken, I said to him: 'Sir, I've often thought that we've met before, and it seems to me that this isn't the first time that you've offered me a cigarette!'

'I wish,' he replied, 'that we really had known each other for a long time, because I like you. I have no intention of releasing you from my service. I have chosen you for a number of important assignments. You are to get to know the world and describe it for me. I am sending you to a foreign land. A revolution is going on. A true hell seems to have broken out there, and because you have an eye for this hell, you will go there.'

'You have a better eye yourself!' I said.

'No,' said he, 'I will first learn of hell only after my death. However, let us forget the various departments of the next world so long as I live. I shall give you money and you will go, and you will report to me everything that you have seen.'

Since I was now driven by curiosity as I had previously been driven by vanity, I took the money and went to the country in which hell had broken out.

I wrote from there about everything that I saw. And I saw much.

I lived in one of the great houses that are called hotels. The

Hotel Excelsior was its name, so clearly it was a greatly important hotel. I had money.

Across from my windows stood an old, venerable church, and from my elevated vantage point I could see directly into the belfry of this church.

At a time when cannon were being fired in the town against those of its inhabitants who were deemed rebels, I heard the bells tolling loudly, and I watched from my window as the heavy bells swung.

So I went into the church and asked the sexton, who was pulling the ropes, why and for what purpose he was ringing the bells.

'The minister gave me the order,' said the sexton.

I went to the minister, who was sitting in his room reading the Bible.

It was already night-time. On the priest's table a lamp was burning under a green shade. I heard the booming of the bells near by and the cannon thundering in the distance.

He was a gentle man, the minister. He had a smooth face, kindly eyes and a pleasant voice.

'I can't hear the sound of the cannon,' he told me. 'I've ordered that the bells are to be rung whenever they begin to fire the cannon.'

'Your Reverence,' said I, 'are you perhaps the brother of my master, who has sent me here? For I believe that he would have acted the same way as you!'

'No,' said the minister, 'I don't know your master.'

And he began once more to read the Bible.

I remained in the service of the master who ruled over the thousand-tongued messengers, whose tongues themselves manufactured the news. And he sent me here and there in many directions wherever anything happened and there was unrest. There was unrest everywhere in the world.

THE PLACE OF PEACE

> From now on, his love is to be found wherever culture and books
> rule; no longer does he divide the cosmos by countries, rivers,
> and seas, no longer according to race and class; he recognizes only
> two classes now: the aristocracy of learning and the mind as the
> upper world and the plebs and barbarism as the lower.
> – Stefan Zweig, *Erasmus of Rotterdam*

But I also came to a peaceful place in a peaceful town. Here
delegates from all the restless nations in all the restless parts of
the world had convened to consider in what way the tranquillity of
the world might be restored. That is to say, they did not mean the
actual tranquillity of the world but the state of unrest that ruled the
world, which seemed to them to be a state of peace and tranquillity.
These delegates of the various peoples did not wish to bring real
peace into the world but, rather, to make the conflict that dominated
the world feel so natural that the world would begin to believe it
was actual peace. This demonstrated to me that their minds were
truly confused. The Antichrist had so confused their minds that
they mistook conflict for peace and strove to consolidate it. They
resembled doctors who cannot let a terminally ill man die because
law and conscience forbid them to do so, and they persuade the
sick man that, because he hasn't died, he must therefore be
healthy. The world, however, is like a sick man who imagines he

must be healthy because he is being kept alive. And the place of which I am speaking, peaceful although it was, none the less resembled a battlefield, namely one on which doctors are battling death, and I could smell the same odour that arises at medical consultations, for I was actually standing at the sickbed of a terminally ill world that could not be allowed to die. There was a stench of camphor and iodoform, and just as real doctors speak in Latin so did these doctors of the world, and the sick patient could understand only every tenth word of what they said.

I came to this peaceful place upon the instruction of my employer, the Master of a Thousand Tongues, and as I could understand Latin I knew what the doctors were talking about. I was prepared to report everything I had heard and understood, and so I wrote it down and sent it to my employer. But he then took one of the numerous red, blue and green pencils that lay on his desk not so he might write with them but only that he could strike with them, and he thus struck out all the truths from my reports so that the world didn't learn it was terminally ill and was simply not being allowed to die. And thus he acted like the anxious relative of a deathly ill patient. The terminally ill patient is not told that he is dying. He might in that case die sooner, and it would be claimed that the doctors were incompetent.

Among these doctors of the world I found some whose appearance was such that I was tempted to believe I had seen them before. Sometimes, when one or another of them gave me a cigarette, I got the feeling that at the next moment he would also offer me chocolate. He did not do this, however, for he believed I would then recognize him. And these were the most gentle of the convened doctors. And they were so affable and they knew their patient so well that they understood exactly in which of its limbs and body parts the world was weakest. And it was towards the weakest limbs and organs that they were the most gentle, almost gentler than they were by nature.

So, for example, they discussed in a special commission, although here also they spoke Latin, in what way one might assist the coloured races.

The coloured races – that is to say, in the language of this world, those people whose skin colour is not white but brown, black, yellow or reddish. And, although it should be clear and obvious to everyone that the colour of the human skin is as much intended by God as is the human face or the human form, people still believe that whatever their own colour might be, it is just through this colour that God has distinguished them from people of other colours. Whereas it is clearly written that God created man in His image: man, not his colour. He created grey, black, greenish and reddish trees and plants, and they are all trees and plants. He created grey, brown, red and yellow animals; silvery and golden fish; greenish, reddish and bluish waters; blue, green, silver and gold stars; clouds in all colours that our human eye can recognize and distinguish – yet they are all clouds, stars, waters, animals, fish and birds. And if the black raven could speak with reason and not only with its tongue it would not deny that the reddish-green parrot, although it is not black, is a bird like he, the black raven. This is because the animals, waters, clouds and plants are not delivered up to the Serpent, the First Serpent, the Antichrist. We humans, however, are delivered up to him, and thus a white man says he is superior to a black man and vice versa; whereas anyone of any colour would think it insanity if he heard someone say that a green room is better than a red one – *is* better and not that one person or another *likes* it more. Or if someone were to say the red leaves of autumn *are* better than the green ones of spring – and not that he *likes* them more.

And instead of thanking God for creating man in His image, and truly with the divine magnanimity that we praise in Him, in all possible colours, people deny Him by the very fact that they say He did not create everyone in His image. We do not know the colour of Adam, the first human. Since, however, in the history of creation not only does every word have its obvious meaning but also every omission, we must assume that Adam's skin colour would have been mentioned if God had intended to give a preference to any particular one. But we do not speak of the colour of the first man from whom we are all descended any more than we speak of his mother tongue, his race or his nationality. Rather, we assume that he, who was the founder of mankind, contained within himself the source of all languages, all races, all peoples and all the variations of skin colour. And Adam was the crown of creation. God Himself took a full five long days to make him, and these were not our short human days, from sun-up to sun-down, but vast in extent, according to the time reckoning of eternity not of the calendar. It is a hardly comprehensible honour that God bestowed upon us in devoting such a long period of thought to us. Many differences distinguish we humans from the animals. But the most important is that God gave Himself five days to create man and that He breathed His breath into him alone – just humans, not humans of one or another colour. This is the only permissible pride we may feel that cannot be called a sin. But it is a double sin that we commit when we pervert our just pride at being people into a vile pride at being white, black, brown or red people. And as it is already deemed as disgraceful in our everyday world when an unworthy fellow denies his grandfather, so should it be a mortal sin and branded as such when a man denies Adam, the ancestor of us all. Thus one denies God Himself with whom our first bond is that He animated Adam with His divine breath.

God created man in his own image. We therefore blasph
Him when we mock or disparage the hooked nose of the Jew, the
slanted eyes of the Mongol or the large lips of the African. Since they
are all human beings, each particular feature and each particular
colour of every human race is to be found in the sublime and
unfathomable countenance of God. Whoever insults the Jew's nose
or the African's lips or the Mongol's eyes or the white man's pallor
therefore insults the nose, the lips, the eyes and the colour of God.
He also defames His breath, which was breathed into the first man.
For in this breath were contained all the virtues of all future people.
Within it were the wondrous singing voice of the African, the
subtlety and also the fervour of the Mongol, the nobility of the
Indian, the intelligence of the Jew – and so forth.

In the Commission on Colours I saw, however, that not only were
the powerful arrogant towards the powerless but that the latter
defended themselves with an equal arrogance towards the powerful.
And because at this time white men happen to be more powerful
than men of other colours, those among them who were still con-
scientious were striving for the emancipation of the coloured
peoples. The Antichrist, however, was already living among both.
And he led the coloured peoples, who were not yet freed, who were
still enslaved by the whites, to mimic their morals and vices and pretensions. And so the brown and black and yellow men all lived apart,
ate and drank apart. The brown men were proud of their brownness,
the black of their blackness and the yellow of their yellowness. It
was obvious that they did not regard themselves first and foremost
as people, but rather as *coloured* people. They also demanded in all
their speeches and uprisings not so much the liberties that truly characterize human dignity as the unworthy ones that power usurps as
its prerogative. What they demanded, and what they ever repeated,
was 'We want to be masters in our own country.' Yes, they wanted

to be masters, nothing else. And in their own country. Instead of saying 'We want to be people in all the countries of the world,' they said
that they wanted to be masters in their own countries. And I thereby
recognized that the Antichrist was in control among them also.

I said this to one of them, a man with kind eyes and an agreeable voice. He came from India. He replied: 'Since you came to us
with violence and trickery and brought us your alcohol and syphilis,
but we didn't come to you with trickery and violence, to defend
ourselves we must speak with the words that you have taught us
and fight with the weapons that you use.'

To which I answered that he had spoken much foolishness in
two phrases but that that he had revealed his great folly mainly
through the use of a couple of little words – namely 'your' and
'you'. Since I had unfortunately not seen his country I couldn't
object to his regarding mine as he regarded his own. I also looked
upon his country as I looked upon mine. If, perhaps, I were to bring
some disease or other evil into his country I could no doubt assume
that there were other diseases and evils that were common and
native to that place. For we are all a mixture of virtue and sin. And
it was precisely because all men were comprised in the same way
of virtue and sin, strength and weakness, goodness and malice,
disease and health, that I couldn't comprehend why every country
should be jealous of exactly those frailties, evils and diseases that
it imagined were special and peculiar to itself. As far as I was concerned, at that moment, as we conversed one man to another,
was he, I asked him, speaking with me or with my skin colour?
For he used the plural pronoun when speaking to me, although
I was only one person.

At this, he replied that he had become used to it because it
was the people of my colour who had begun by addressing people
of his colour in this way, saying 'you' and 'your' to them.

'Let us assume,' I said to him, 'that there was a certain town, and in this town lived a great many murderers. Would you therefore address each citizen of the town as "you murderers" or say "among you murderers"? And,' said I further, 'I have read that in your country live many wise men. Am I to address everyone in your country as "you wise men"?'

'I have seldom met anyone of your type,' he said, thinking to compliment me.

With this I recognized him and told him that he seemed to be the twin brother of my employer – the wise Master of a Thousand Tongues. And then I said bluntly: 'The Antichrist walks in your country also. And that is worse than syphilis.'

He seemed not to understand. He said nothing. As, however, he was concerned to reconcile me he searched, very much as the Antichrist would, not for a subject that we might both like but for one that he thought I would hate. And he said: 'The worst are the half-breeds.'

'No,' I said, 'the worst are those who would think and say such a thing. For we are all people, and when people come together with each other it is natural and the will of God that everything should happen between them that can occur between human beings. They can speak to one another, they can hate one another, they can love one another and they can sleep with one another. Love between a red man and a yellow woman is natural. For if nature didn't wish this love to exist it would prevent them from bearing fruit. Since children spring from such a love these children are neither better nor worse than any others. When, however, two women or two men of the same colour love each other, this process goes against nature, even though people must obey the particular ways of their own bodies. There certainly exist within creation many phenomena that are subject not to the general laws of creation but to others of a special and remarkable kind. We have no right to condemn them. Neither do we have the right to see them as natural. That would be as if those who were born blind were considered to have the same sight as those who are not blind, merely because it is Nature itself that made them blind and not an accident. In this world, however, where the Antichrist blinds even those who can see, it comes to pass that people say: "An unnatural love between two white men is better and nobler than a natural love between a white man and a yellow woman." And this is a twofold sin. For the infirm must bear their infirmities humbly, and a cripple cannot direct how the healthy should run. I know a man who has sexual intercourse with goats, but won't give his hand to a Chinese man.' Another person who heard me speak thusly came to me and said he could understand everything that I was thinking. For, although he came from a distant land, namely Japan, he was also in the service of a Master of a Thousand Tongues. And, like myself, he went everywhere that there was unrest in the world.

'I'm older than you,' said he. 'I offer you this advice: never again speak as you did just now. In reality, there are other cares in your country, in mine, in all the countries where people live. There is a great outcry of the tormented of all races and within each race. To those who are poor and downtrodden, the colour of people's skin is immaterial. He who has nothing to eat feels hungry. He who is beaten bleeds. The educated folk who say "We want to be masters in our own country" are actually already masters in their own countries. All they want to do is drive out of their countries those people who share the mastery with them. It is only the masters who come to these conferences; and we, who are sent here by the masters. There's no point in getting too excited. Look at what happened to me. I was a soothsayer. I was never able to tell a lie. Only since I have been hired and paid to report the truth do I lie. And one day you also will act just as I do. Even if you refuse to lie, you will find your truths so disfigured that you would rather have lied yourself. Fare thee well!' This he said and left me.

THE RED EARTH

Erasmus loved many of the things that we love; literature and
philosophy, books and artworks, languages and peoples, and
without distinction among them all, the whole of mankind . . .
And there was only one thing on earth that he truly . . . hated –
fanaticism. – Stefan Zweig, *Erasmus of Rotterdam*

Then I went to the country where, so I had been told, there was no
longer an outcry from the poor and downtrodden; people were concerned to let truth, justice and reason shine forth; gold, the metal
of the Antichrist, had been conquered; and people had a natural
respect for every single human life, and each was sacred.

So I came to the capital city of this land. It is an old town, a
pretty, expansive city with many hundreds of old churches. If one
looks down upon this city from a high vantage point one sees the
green arches and cupolas scattered like giant jewels between flat
and pointed roofs. Each century seems to have contributed to the
making of this city's jewels.

I visited many of these cupolas and the churches over which they
vault their arches, and I saw that in many of the churches people no
longer prayed and that the bells had been removed from the belfries
and the crosses from the cupolas and from the walls inside.

'We have placed God at a distance,' I was told by a number of
people. 'Let others copy us if they please! We have, as you can see

for yourself, not only abolished wealth, gold, the emperor and the executioner but swept Heaven clean of all the filth that had collected there during the course of history. Now the earth is clean and the sky is empty.'

And so the deed was done. They had taken up two brooms in their hands, one for sweeping the earth and one for sweeping the heavens. And they had even given the brooms names. The one was called Revolution, and the other was called Human Reason.

Yet there were many in this land who did not approve of one or the other or even both of these brooms.

Some of these people could truly believe that the earth was now clean because they could see the earth.

But as they could not see Heaven they mistrusted the broom that was called Human Reason.

'If you mistrust your own reason,' the sweepers informed them, 'it's because you don't have enough of it.'

'But maybe,' replied the others, 'you trust reason so much because you yourselves possess so little of it. And perhaps you have more than us, but it's possible there exists something other than human reason, namely a divine reason. And your own superior reason is no better than our poor reason at recognizing this divine reason. You think you know, but we believe.'

'And even if you are right,' replied the sweepers, 'and even if there is really a divine reason that is superior to ours, we still cannot let it prevail any longer. For you must remember that our last oppressors appealed to this unknowable divine reason and that they oppressed us in its name.'

'We don't deny that,' answered the wiser among the faithful. 'It was the sin of the oppressors that they brazenly proclaimed that they alone (and not us) could know the intentions of the divine will. And if they could really do so then it was a double sin to oppress us by appealing to this knowledge. For, as minimal as our knowledge is, yet all the faithful know this one thing, that God doesn't want oppression. And we were also foolish when we believed that the powerful knew more about divine purposes than did we. That was our fault. We admit it.

'But at the very least you are guilty of denying something about which you are uncertain – is it there, or isn't it there? Do you know, for example, from whence man comes and to whence he goes? Do you know what happened before your birth and what will happen after your death? Have you already spoken with some-one who is dead or with someone not yet born?'

The sweepers said: 'Even if we could talk with those who aren't yet born or those who have died, we wouldn't do so. We have too much concern about the misery of the living. We don't have as much time as you do. We follow the maxim: *Religion is the opium of the people.*'

'Now,' said the wiser among the faithful, 'although you have no time we can wait. For we have time. We have until the end of time.'

And the faithful went to pray.

But they were not left in peace. It was remarkable that exactly those people who had said they had no time to speak with the dead, even if they could do so, still found time to disturb the faith-ful. They wrote above the image of the Madonna, which was set up before one of the gates of the broom-master's palace, the phrase of their prophet: *Religion is the opium of the people.*

What a saying. Foolish like all sayings that have the strength to wheedle their way into the ears of men, as a popular song might. They are as far removed from wisdom as popular tunes are from real music. One could even turn this saying around, just as the verses of a hit song can be sung backwards without changing the musical sense. In this saying the words do not possess their original meaning but rather an applied one. It is the same with the sound of a popular song. One could turn the sense of the song into its opposite and it would sound just as flattering to the frivolous ear. One could, for example, say *Unbelief is the opium of the people*; or, if one wished, *Opium is the religion of the rich*; or perhaps *The rich are the opium of religion*; or maybe *Those in power are the opium of the people*; or, if one preferred, *The powerful* – and actually the powerful at any particular time and not religion – *are the opium of the people*. The words of a philosopher? Not a chance! It is the slogan of a parliamentarian!

This slogan was written above an image of the Madonna. But, regardless, many people prayed before this image each day. And it was as though they were asking the Mother of God for forgiveness for the slogan that had been placed over her image. And as there were no more rich people left in this country, those who came to kneel and pray before the Mother of God were poor. Poor by birth or had become so – whatever the reason, they were poor. And therefore – the people. The Mother of God was dignified in her apparent helplessness against the power of the catchphrase because she was visibly weak, and all that was left to her was the seemingly insignificant ability to attract those who were poor and mocked, in other words – the people! She promised nothing, she performed no miracles, she gave no speeches, she was mocked, and yet there were people who clung to her and allowed themselves to be persecuted for her sake.

They were all poor. And since, for one must be fair, in this country, everything possible was done for the people under the given circumstances, I asked myself why these poor people still prayed. Just what made them drift towards an unknown force, although they could see that the known powers were eager to help them? They must have been so distressed that they could not speak of it to the known and visible powers. One mother's son was dying, and the doctors in the hospital were powerless against death. The doctors gave him real opium so that he would not suffer, and this was all they could do. A woman wanted to have a child, but enigmatic Nature gave her nothing. Another woman had not wanted to have the child she was carrying, and it pained her that she did not wish to bring it into the world. And there was a man who was weeping over his dead brother, whom the improved conditions of this world could not bring back. Still others were praying simply because their hearts were full. Without any reason. For even though the sweepers had cleared the earth of all kinds of garbage, people's hearts could not be emptied of the inexplicable sorrow that often filled them. If the sweepers had been able, as was certainly their intention, to quench hunger and thirst, to provide shelter for all who had to sleep under the sky, to supply beds and medicine to the sick, crutches to the lame and guide dogs to the blind, there would still remain hearts that needed more, needed something that could never be provided by earthly powers. There are many who prefer unjust love to loveless justice. And they are not happy unless they are both loved and hurt.

For between that which constitutes man's predictable happiness and that which constitutes his unpredictable happiness there is a wide gap that we cannot fill with our logical reasoning. We are made of flesh and spirit. A cat is contented simply with milk and butter, but a man is not satisfied for long after having eaten and drunk. And even if he is given books, taken to the theatre and his curiosity about earthly knowledge satisfied, there will always be a moment in which he asks, like the child he has never ceased to be: 'Why? Why?'

There can be no answer to all of his questions. Not even when he asks: 'Father, why hast Thou forsaken me?'

The people had previously been kept in blinkers. In this country, however, everyone thought that these questions would stop if only satisfactory replies were given to those questions that could be answered for the time being.

Those questions for which an answer could be found began to be placed before the citizens of the country, even when they had no wish to pose such questions themselves.

So the people were taught to pose questions but only those questions for which there was an answer at the ready.

Those questions that could not be answered, even when they were put into words, were left without an answer.

Because the people of this country were believers by nature, and because they had been forcibly kept in ignorance and blindness for many long years before the Revolution, the equally forceful attempt to grant them knowledge and education succeeded in surpassing through so-called natural wonders the supernatural wonders in which they were accustomed to believing.

The people there were kindly people. One could persuade them that the saints in Heaven concerned themselves about a sick cow and a lame calf.

When veterinarians came to treat the sick cattle, it was proved that an ordinary animal doctor could do more than a saint.

In the villages in the southern portion of this great country the people believe, for example, that the prophet Elijah makes thunder, lightning and rain. And when the fields needed a storm, the people prayed to St Elijah.

On the day of this holy one's feast the authorities who had swept Heaven empty decided to prove to the peasants in the villages that storms are not caused by saints. They sent experts to the villages on that very day, equipped with a number of scientific apparatus. These experts showed the people the scientific laws of thunder, lightning and storms.

When the poor people now saw that men could produce storms using machines they stopped (although not all at once) believing in the power of St Elijah.

However, they did begin to believe in the power of the apparatus and the supernatural power of the men who used it. Since it was a dry summer, and the fields could have used a storm, they asked these educated men to create a proper storm.

'This apparatus is too small for all the vast fields,' said the learned men. The people would have to wait until someone built a bigger machine.

This answer, or excuse, was so crafty that I was seized by the desire to speak with such clever men.

I told them that they must have realized that they had lied.

'Naturally we lied!' they replied. 'Because we had to drive Elijah out of the peasants even at the price of a lie. From St Elijah to the Tsar is only one step.' I asked them what then did they believe – that the Tsar had supported the saint or vice versa? And why wasn't it possible to understand an apparatus and also venerate the holy? And were the saints the foes of science? And weren't they aware that it is human nature to replace each saint that has been taken away with a new one? And does the so-called blind faith in a saint have less value than blind faith in a man?

'They don't want a blind faith,' said the learned ones in reply.

'But there is something worse,' I said to them, 'and that is blind knowledge. We have only two eyes to see with. Alas, there is so much to see in the world that we would require a thousand eyes. With our two poor eyes we cannot perceive all these things. And therefore we cannot say that we know all and can teach all. It is just as false to think that our eyes can see everything as it is to close them intentionally so that they can't see anymore. None of us has seen St Elijah. But we don't know whether we haven't seen him because he isn't there or because we are simply unable to see him.'

The gentlemen laughed and said that they had worries other than mine. They would speak with me again later after they had eliminated these other worries from the world.

Because, however, my worries were at their root the same as those of the peasants, I know that these gentlemen were not thinking logically. It is, in any case, easier to persuade the credulous through a scientific apparatus than to argue with believers.

The founder of their world was named Lenin, and after his death they put him into a glass coffin. His body was embalmed and paraffin was injected into his cheeks so that for decades after he will still look as though he is sleeping peacefully, not like a dead man. They set the transparent coffin in the middle of the square behind whose walls is the place where the inheritance of the deceased is administered. Thus any of the citizens and any visitor to the country can look at this dead man who seems only to be asleep.

Many childlike people believe that he really is asleep, and is only resting temporarily.

If one enquires why and on what basis was the dead man embalmed and displayed in a kind of solemn shop window, one soon comes to the conclusion that there were many reasons and a variety of purposes. The sweepers wanted to snatch from eternity at least a part of what belongs to it. And since it is impossible to conquer Death, they wanted at least to conquer the corpse, whose law is decay and not permanence. Thus it is like an ostentatious – but, naturally, at the same time childish – threat to Death, who is shown that his victim can none the less be preserved, like a piece of jewellery that is no longer worn.

To provide visual proof of this was one of the most important goals.

'You have taken him from us,' said the sweepers to Death. 'We will show you, however, that we can keep him. And we will display him to all the world just as he looked during his lifetime.'

If they had been capable of hearing Death's answer, it would have been something like the following: 'Your threat is childish and your pride is foolish. It is my purpose to take from this earth not his face but his life and what you loved – his breath. He is extinguished, like a lamp. I have taken wick and oil. You may keep the vessel. I am not concerned with it. It was his flame that you loved and his light! Why are you now flaunting the miserable vessel that held them? I have already extinguished many great lights, and monuments were built to them. And that is wiser than what you do! For a monument does not deny but rather confirms the law according to which I act. And since it confirms me it conquers me as well. Because a monument, however insignificant, is the sign that the living remember the dead, and it is a terrestrial, inadequate but reverent form of resurrection. However, you don't cause the dead man to be resurrected; you only make his corpse last. You prevent it from decaying. Why shouldn't a corpse turn into dust and ashes? Did men come from paraffin and wax to become paraffin and wax once again? If you have as much respect for the dead man as you say, don't you understand that he should not be exhibited the way a barber displays wax busts with wigs? Why do you so proudly show off for me – for Death? You have snatched nothing from me. Instead, you have detracted from your own dignity – your own dignity as well as the dignity of your dead.'

But, as I said, the sweepers were unable to hear the voice of Death.

Neither was he speaking to them. He was talking to himself with a compassion-filled voice.

In the vicinity of the city lived a righteous man, and I was advised to seek him out. He was surely one of the thirty-six righteous men – of whom it was written that on their account, and on their account alone, the world will continue to exist – who live scattered around the earth, their significance and influence unrecognized by mankind, expert in interpreting the language of animals, the song of the birds and the silence of the fish.

So I went to this righteous man.

He lived meagrely but so alone that the confinement of his room was no longer confinement but rather a wide expanse. He was surrounded with the regal splendour of solitude in which all earthly misery was lost like a speck of dust in a strong, sweeping wind.

They had treated him unjustly, for it is written that the righteous must suffer.

In this, however, the righteous man is like God, and this grace was granted him that he might serve not only as an image of God, as we all are but as an exalted image of our Creator. The righteous man is never unjust, and he treats you and I the same as he treats the unjust. It is only because we are, in truth, incapable of recognizing a righteous man that we say he *forgives* his enemies.

The righteous man who is the topic of this discourse had been thrown into prison. And it was claimed that he had wanted to eliminate the liberty of the people; he, who hated slavery and loved liberty, and who lived only to ensure that there would exist only free men and no more slaves.

It only became evident that he was one of the thirty-six righteous when his righteousness was not recognized and he was thrown into prison under the accusation of being unrighteous.

Accordingly, he bore imprisonment, hunger and beatings with the dignity of the righteous. He was lonely in prison. He was surrounded always by the strong armour of solitude, which is stronger even than iron.

This armour of solitude came between him and the violence that struck him, so that sometimes he almost wished that the blows were truly painful.

I spoke with this man. I told him that I could see the signs of the Antichrist in his great, vast and beautiful country; that I feared the Antichrist alone had triumphed.

'He hasn't triumphed,' said the righteous man. 'He has only left here, there and everywhere so strong an imprint of his evil fingers that we are tempted to believe that all new creations are the work of his hands. But it isn't true. They bear the impression of his fingers only where he touched them.

'But there is something else that you cannot see,' the righteous man went on, 'because you are a new guest to our country. The Antichrist didn't emerge with the new era in this country but many years ago under the old regime. Clever as he was, he first tempted the standard-bearers, not the rebels. Not those who sought reforms but those whose jobs were to preserve the status quo. First he took up residence in the churches and then in the houses of the masters. For that is the method by which you may unmistakably know him, and it is an error, a mistake of the world, when it believes he can be recognized because he provokes and incites the humiliated and enslaved. That would be foolish – and the Antichrist is cunning. He doesn't inspire the oppressed to rebel but inspires the masters to oppress. He doesn't make rebels, rather he makes tyrants. He knows that if first he introduces tyranny, rebellion will soon come on its own. Thus his gain is twofold. For he forces the just, who would otherwise resist him, into his service. He doesn't persuade the slaves that they should be masters, rather he first makes the masters his slaves. Then, when they have entered into his service he forces them to debase the powerless, the poor, the hardworking, the humble and the righteous into slavery. The wretched and the humble then revolt against the powerful, and the reasonable and the just rise up against stupidity and injustice. The just put weapons into the hands of the wretched. They must do it, for they are the righteous ones.

'It is therefore false for the people of the world to say that the Antichrist leads the rebels. On the contrary; he leads those who wish for the status quo. Because his nature prevents it he cannot approach the sufferers as easily as he can approach the powerful. He who suffers is better equipped against evil than he who rules, gives orders and enjoys. The world is founded upon justice. This is the special cunning of the Antichrist, that he disguises himself in the mask of a rebel to prevent immediate recognition by his opponents, so that they seek him in the ranks of the rebels while he is actually raging and wreaking havoc among the ranks of the masters.

'It is written that the righteous must suffer. It is true that all those who suffer are not necessarily righteous, but if one day I were given the mission of finding righteous men I would search for them in the endless ranks of the suffering. It is they who are first tasked with restoring justice in this world. And while they are striving to re-establish the justice that has been distorted by the Antichrist and his slaves, the tyrants, they must be placed under the suspicion that they are driven by the Antichrist. It is precisely by this that I recognize them as righteous. For their suffering is twofold. They suffer under the violence of the unjust and under the reproach of the just.'

'But they won't recognize God,' I said, 'and they claim that they themselves are gods.'

'They must never have known God,' replied the righteous man. 'A human power had intervened between God and themselves, and just as the Antichrist first made tyrants of the masters before he led their victims to revolt, so he first made liars of the priests before he compelled the believers to deny God. Since the priests had blanketed God with lies, those who deny Him – or, as they call themselves, the godless ones – aren't denying God but actually the false image that has been handed down to them.

'Weren't they told that God wanted murder, injustice, tyranny, gold and the whip? And, what is still worse, that he was, nevertheless, the God of Love? And didn't the mediators of God cause the bells, the golden tongues of faith, to be rung to celebrate the hour at which the black jaws of cannon, the mouths of death, were opened?'

'Above the statue of the Madonna,' I said, 'before which hundreds of people pray every day, they have placed the phrase: *Religion is the opium of the people.* What a saying!'

'A lying and a stupid saying,' said the righteous man. 'However, is it worse than the motto that escapes from the mouths of our priests: *Faith is honey for the people*? It is the lying echo to this lying saying. People can't shout lies into the world and expect the echo to shout back the truth.

'So it is, my friend! The rotten fruit falls from the tree, the dry leaf withers, the dead spring dries up, the empty cloud delivers no rain, the gentle wind brings no storm, the empty heart is devoid of goodness, and a liar never speaks the truth. A steady throne won't hold a weak emperor, the ruler who has become a slave of the Devil can no longer be a master, and the subject of this ruler is no longer a subject. A slave of the Devil can no longer rule. It is the lying mediator of God who denies Him and not the defrauded believer. It was God's mediators whom the Antichrist first seduced. Then the godless ones came as a matter of course.

'Even one who calls himself godless is not really without God. One who denies God by enveloping Him in lies is worse than one who simply calls himself godless. So if a man tells me that he does not believe in God, then I am sad for him. But if someone tells me that he believes in God but that injustice is justice, then I curse him.

'Our people in this country,' continued the righteous man, 'deny the existence of God, but they don't tell lies about Him. And it is, in truth, sinful to say that God doesn't exist. It is more sinful – for sin, like hell, has countless gradations – to falsify God and defraud men with His falsified image. Therein lies the sin.'

I took leave of the righteous man and journeyed through the country.

And I saw that there had been built new houses, new monuments, new factories, new hospitals, new playhouses, new cinemas, new schools, high schools and colleges for older people who could not read or write.

People were working in the factories, people were living in the houses, people were healing and dying in the hospitals, people were acting in the theatres, people were teaching and learning in the schools.

Everywhere, even when it wasn't in writing, I sensed the phrase that is just as foolish as the one that says religion is opium – namely, the saying: *Education is power*.

In this saying, too, the words do not have their original meaning but rather an applied one. One could say, if one desired: *Power is education*; or perhaps: *Education is weakness*; or, if one preferred: *Power makes weak* – or *strong*, depending on the situation.

After I had visited the righteous man I tried to see a little with his righteous eyes, and I realized that such foolish sayings were bound to come into being because those who had been powerful and also uneducated for so long believed that education, or this or that thing of which they had been deprived for that long, created and maintained the might of the mighty.

Whereas this phrase was actually false, if only because those in power are by no means educated; on the contrary, they are uneducated.

It is also childish for people to make education palatable by saying that it lends power.

It is similar to how children are foolishly promised sweets if they will be obedient and hardworking. They are led astray by the suggestion that obedience and hard work are not rewards in themselves but produce a reward for the tongue and palate, which have nothing to do with dutifulness and work.

Thus, because of this stupid motto, the people who were powerless for so long were led like children to believe that learning brings something other than the true reward, namely, an education.

It might, by the way, have been merely an idea of the Antichrist to persuade the people that they would obtain power.

Were it not an idea of the Antichrist the phrase would have gone something like this: *Education makes us more just than we had been*. For the world is built upon justice and not upon power. When the people, as if they were children, were promised the sweet poison of power, they began, with all the boundless enthusiasm that is only common to children, to absorb education. Since, however, the stuff of teaching and knowledge, which they call education, does not always contain the ultimate truth but only a temporary truth that may be contradicted or rendered obsolete at any second, the good people learned a mixture of truth and lies –

and what they learned the most rapidly was to confuse one with the other.

For human knowledge is not divine truths but rather the pathways to reach these truths. Some are crooked, others are straight; some lead to the goal, others lead astray. When the real goal, namely truth and justice, is not expressly named but is alleged to be power, one cannot know whether he is travelling a straight path or a crooked one.

Therefore, the people in this country are going astray despite their diligent learning.

Those who could not read or write now read and write enthusiastically, day and night. Now it hardly matters whether a man can decipher or write letters, only what letters he deciphers or writes, and what meaning results. And if this yields a false or petty result, it is worse than if the people had not learned their letters at all. For in that case education is indeed not power (not even power) but only weakness and slavery. And the Antichrist leads people to learn their letters and promises them power only that the people grow even *more* powerless.

The people in this country are, however, very proud of all the knowledge that the human world has acquired so far. In this knowledge they see truth. And although they have learned that yesterday's knowledge is contradicted by today's, they still firmly believe in the knowledge of today – as though there were no tomorrow and no day after tomorrow. Therefore they have more respect for one of yesterday's machines than for a truth that might emerge tomorrow or the next day.

Just as some peoples worship idols, knowing full well that these have been made of gold or wood by human hands, the people in this land worship machines, thus they too worship idols.

The people worship both the machine builders *and* the

machines – just as the Children of Israel worshipped Aaron and yet danced around the golden calf that they had seen him create with their very eyes.

When people are taught that God does not exist, they will make themselves idols.

It is the same today as it was five thousand years ago. When Moses, who announced the God of the burning bush, disappeared for a forty-day period on the peak of Mount Sinai the Children of Israel demanded the golden calf.

If their St Elijah is taken away, they dance around a piece of scientific equipment.

And if they can no longer go about in processions, they will dance around a tractor.

I am far from wishing to disparage the tractor and praise the ox.

For, as I have already said at the beginning, the curse of God that we should plough the earth in the sweat of our brows was alleviated by the grace of reason, which allowed us to invent the tractor with which to plough the earth.

But we have as little reason to be proud of the tractor as we have to be proud of the ox. Perhaps there was a time in which fools worshipped the plough and its inventor. God gave us the ox and the plough as well as the tractor. He alone must we worship.

If, however, we regard His gifts and mercies as human merits and, worse still, as proofs against His existence, then this happens at the command of the Antichrist.

The scientific apparatus with which we can recreate thunder and lightning was also given to us by God, just as he gave us the actual thunder and lightning. For he gave us the power of reason through which the machine was invented.

Thunder and lightning, the blessings of rain and corn and fruit on the tree, the terror of hail, in short, life and death – these are given to us by the power that we call the Lord.

He also gives us understanding of how we may perfect His blessing and lighten His curse.

Instead of praising Him, we think that we see in the consequences of His mercy proof that He does not exist.

Thus, we are like the beggar and scrounger who was once given alms by a rich man, alms that later bore fruit so that he himself became rich. Then, however, he said: 'The rich man didn't give me anything. I alone have made myself rich.'

I know of no other kind of rich man.

In this country they strive to re-establish the worth of all people, without distinction. By this I recognized the reign of the Antichrist, even in this place where they value all people equally.

The worth of man, who was created in God's image, cannot be established where it is regarded as strictly his own worth and not as a divine grace. They may build houses in this country as tall as those in America, and set up a new Hollywood, an Unholywood, where the salvation of actors is located, and a thousand new factories, and a thousand hospitals, a thousand schools small and large, yet they will not dwell easily in the houses, no shadows will find salvation, the products of the factories will have no excellence, those dying in the hospitals will not be cured and in the schools no scholars will become wise . . . without grace, without that which we call 'grace'.

THE HOME OF THE SHADOWS

In the human face of today, nothing has grown; everything within has been drawn out or thrust out of the surface – and wonders that it still exists . . .

The transference to the mechanical sphere of that which is mobile, hurried, provisional, fleeting in the modern face – this is the cinematic face. The cinema could only be invented because of the modern face. Confronted with the monumentality of the human face as it used to be, the movements on the cinema screen would never have dared to combine together into a picture resembling a face. They would have separated and become dispersed before this monumentality. – Max Picard, *The Human Face*

I went to the country where the houses are built so high that they scrape the sky. They are, therefore, called skyscrapers.

The land is large and spacious but expensive. Because of this, they did not build one house next to another but one house *over* the other, for the air is still free there.

Thus the people prefer to scrape the sky rather than nestle close to the earth.

And through this their arrogance continues to grow.

In this country, when one has a yellow or black skin colour, he may not sit in the same room with a man whose colour is white.

In this country there are thousands of churches. But in these churches money is collected with the help of devotions. The people carry God in the mouth and speak of God as if he were a rich and distinguished uncle who raises one's worth when one mentions that one is His nephew.

Many people in this country are, in fact, not the Children of God but nephews of God – the nephew heirs of God.

The poor ask Him for money, and the rich ask Him for even more money.

And in this country God often acts as though He really were a wealthy uncle. To many of the poor He gives money, and to many of the rich He gives even more money.

He enlarges the chimneys of the factories and increases the alms of the beggars; and He often hardens hearts that are already hard and breaks those hearts that are soft; He gives to those who have while taking away from those who have not.

These are His special laws in this country. People's worth is grounded in power. Liberty stands as a statue *outside* the gates; they have ejected her. And she has turned to stone.

I went to Hollywood, to Unholywood, to the place where hell rages, that is to say, where people are the *doppelgängers* of their own shadows. This is the source of all the shadows in the world, the Hades that sells its shadows for money, the shadows of both the living and of the dead who appear on all the screens of the world. The owners of usable shadows assemble here and sell them for money and are treated as holy ones or saints, as befits the importance of their shadows.

The living girls and boys around the world who see these shadows take on their walk, their facial expression, their form and attitude. That is why one often comes across men and women, actual people in the street, who are not the *doppelgängers* of their own shadows like the actors of the cinema, but even less, namely the *doppelgängers* of strangers' shadows.

It is thus a Hades, which not only sends its shadows up to the surface but also converts those who live on the surface and have not sold their shadows into *doppelgängers* of these shadows.

This is Hollywood.

Hell rages. There is a rush of shadow-players' managers, shadow-dealers and shadow-brokers, shadow-arrangers (who are called directors), shadow-conjurors and shadow-renters. There are even those who sell their voices to the shadows of other people who speak a different language.

I also saw there, namely in the factories that buy shadows, about twenty people sitting in large offices, each seated before a telephone. And every two or three minutes a couple of the apparatus would buzz and the men would take the receivers in their hands and say 'Nothing!' And that means: no work.

For people call the shadow-factories every day wanting to sell their shadows. And because there are so many of them who want to offer their shadows, the factories had to engage twenty men to say no. And they say 'Nothing!' every three minutes. The whole day long.

They say nothing else.

So numerous are those in this country who thirst to sell their shadows.

And these are the owners not of ordinary shadows like yours and mine but of remarkable shadows. One man is a giant, another a hunchback, a third a dwarf, a fourth has the face of a horse or a donkey, a fifth can climb like an ape, a sixth can dance on stilts, a seventh on a rope and so on. Others are *doppelgängers* of famous men and can occasionally be used in historical films, and they are therefore double and triple *doppelgängers*. They are not only the *doppelgängers* of their own shadows but also of those of other shadows, which are, strange to say, also their own. Some look like Napoleon or Caesar. So they sell the shadows of their noses, which aren't their own noses at all but those of the famous dead. If these particular noses don't happen to be needed, then one of the twenty naysayers answers no. But if one such nose shadow does happen to be needed, then the yeasayers answer, people who sit in another office also in front of telephones. In the plazas and streets stand many statues of famous men, just as in other cities. In all the other cities of the world, however, statues have no other purpose than to bear witness to the fame of those they portray. But in this city, many of the statues have the job of proclaiming and praising various wares. For example, many famous personalities can be seen in stone and marble or copper and bronze, drinking a cup of cheap and tasty coffee or sucking on cough drops to fight hoarseness. And, whereas in this city the shadows of living men are taken together with their animation, such that the original owner becomes the shadow of his own shadow, the dead statues are supplied with the needs of living people. It may therefore truly be said that in this city, which is inhabited by nothing but shadows, only the statues are people – tasteless, it is true, but people all the same.

Just as the people are shadows and the statues are people, the plants in this city are statues. The palms of Hollywood, for example, don't grow in the soil in which they appear to be rooted but are merely fixed in like statues. They are plants with bases instead of roots. But, whereas statues for the most part stay in the same location for a long time, this is by no means the case with the palms. For the people who rent the palms carry them first to one garden, next to another, and while their characteristic of being fixed into soil makes them similar to the statues, the fact that they change residences makes them resemble fleeting shadows. So it is that some of the most immobile things on earth, namely trees, become nearly as fleeting as the most fleeting phenomena on earth, namely shadows. Moreover, even the palms are now and then called upon to give up their shadows for the screen. And as they are capable of wandering from place to place it can be said of them, as it can also be said of men, that they are the *doppelgängers* of their own shadows. The natural shadow that they cast in their quality as trees becomes the *doppelgänger* of its shadow.

Shadows of clouds and of cloud shadows are also purchased by these factories, which use them whenever a suitable occasion arises. Sometimes men and women arrive who were able to photograph clouds from hardly accessible mountains or clouds in other dangerous locales. And these people are able to sell their cloud shadows to the factories for a designated price.

And just as lives can be turned into shadows, so can death. For in many films the shadows must die. And if it is very difficult to live according to the special laws of the shadow-world, it is much more difficult to die according to those laws. It is so difficult that a genuine death could never be harder.

For I have seen a shadow-master make the *doppelgänger* of a lovely shadow die nineteen times before he declared her death to be genuine and true. He required that her shadow must die not only beautifully but also in vanity. So she lay down and exposed her legs, the pretty *doppelgängers* of leg shadows. The shadow-master was the same one who had displayed the bathing Egyptian girls and the dead soldiers many years before, when I was a boy, arousing our lust, which is directed as much towards the horrors of death as it is towards living flesh.

The people in this city regard death in the same way they regard birth.

When a child is born, it awakes in its mother the hope that it will become a suitable, well-paid shadow.

For, in fact, it sometimes happens that an infant delivers up its tiny shadow and its voice to the screen.

In this city live many devout shadow-worshippers. As they are not content merely to worship shadows, all their thoughts and hopes are directed towards catching a glimpse of, speaking to, embracing or applauding the *doppelgängers* of the shadows they adore. These worshippers are unaware that the originators of the shadows are only *doppelgängers*. The worshippers believe that the actors are yet masters of themselves and of their shadows. And just as many lovers of books and literature have a yearning to see the authors of their favourite works in the flesh, so the shadow-worshipper also wants to see, hear and touch the supposedly living actors. However, they merely encounter the shadows of the famous and beloved shadows.

None the less, even those who are only the shadows of the celebrated and beloved shadows imagine that they are quite alive, like all other people. They are so maintained and strengthened in this conceit by the adoration of their worshippers that a *doppelgänger* of his beloved shadow becomes very unhappy if he is not greeted as he was the day before or if one of his colleagues is greeted more cordially than he.

This vanity and this jealousy nearly led me to believe that these shadows of shadows are somehow human.

On other occasions, however, I was persuaded that they are very different from the rest of mankind.

For example, I saw that women who were pregnant were forbidden to sell their shadows any more.

So they left the shadow-factory, without a word. This seemed to them quite natural.

When pregnant women are shown in films, they are played by non-pregnant women who place a pillow under their clothes and over their wombs. And, as the manmade and moveable palms are preferred to the genuine and rooted palms, the padding is preferred to the pregnant womb.

It is, by the way, wondrous that the *doppelgänger* of a shadow should still possess the natural ability to become pregnant, sometimes even from the embrace of the *doppelgänger* of another shadow.

In this, however, let us recognize the immeasurable goodness of God.

His unfathomable benevolence calls the female shadow to the life of motherhood. Because she has become a living person, because of what is, in her case, the twofold wonder of motherhood, she can no longer play a role – in the actual sense of this word – in the world of shadows. And they chase her out of the gates of the shadow-factory.

I will take this opportunity to mention that in all the countries of the world that are viewed as civilized, the laws of humanity and religion forbid a woman to have the ripening fruit of her body removed.

If I had the power, in the name of divine or earthly justice, to issue decrees, I would outlaw the shadow-factories of Hollywood, if only because they compel women to have the ripening fruit extracted from their bodies.

It grievously astonishes me that ecclesiastical and secular legislators do not know, or do not notice, the inhuman laws of the shadow-factories.

In all the countries of this civilized world a hungry beggar woman is thrown in prison if she has an abortion.

A shadow-manufacturer, however, who causes pregnant women to get abortions, is not sent to prison.

God sees all this. And He will judge the lawmakers as He will judge the shadow-manufacturers. But He will not judge the beggar women.

The Lord will not judge the poor. Nor will He, unlike the lawmakers of this world, in any way judge the destitute who sneak into houses, into strangers' houses.

Such poor I have seen in Hollywood, too. There the poor also sell their shadows. Only there they are not called poor but 'extras'.

And it happens that for one shadow-show or another, many shadow-people are wanted, for example to dwell in a wonderful palace.

They aren't allowed to live in the palace as real people but only as people's shadows or shadow-people.

Once their shadows have been sold they cannot stay in the palace any longer.

It happens that many of the poor who are extras in Hollywood have no shelter for the night.

And, although they have sold their shadows that these shadows may sleep in the palace, they, as *doppelgängers* of their shadows, may not spend the night in this palace. They aren't Roman legionaries, Nubian slaves, armoured knights, janissaries or Crusaders any longer. They are poor homeless people. They call them in this city 'extras'.

Even truth here is nothing but a shadow. After I had seen this city I knew that it – and it alone – was the true capital of this great country, and I had no desire to see any other cities or villages in this land.

It is true that the leader of the country lived in another town.

It is also true that those who had wealth or engaged in business lived in yet another, but Hollywood was the capital. This city, I had come to realize, was the capital not only of the country but of the entire world.

For it is the capital city of the shadows, and it is shadows that rule the world.

All the shadows have their residence in Hollywood. Yes, when I left the city and came to other cities my eyes no longer believed the reality of the things and people they saw in these other cities. If I came across a skyscraper, I imagined it had only been erected for a week's duration so that its shadow might be projected on to the screen for a particular film in which a skyscraper was required.

And, in fact, someone told me that this particular building was about to be torn down and another near by had been constructed just a week before.

As quick and fleeting as shadows, and more transient than the clouds they touch, are the buildings in this country.

The actors are also removed, for people have no use for memories.

I saw kind people in this country as well, but people without time.

Just as the shadows take up no space, so the people in this country have no time.

Goodness, however, requires both time and space.

Even truth in this country is a shadow.

The laws of truth are proclaimed from the capital of the shadows.

It is the truth of shadows and not of people.

Yet even in this country I met a just man. He urged me to have patience and not to be so hasty as the shadows I was condemning.

'This country,' said the just man, 'will perhaps give over all of its shadows and skyscrapers to other countries and itself arrive at life and truth. Perhaps the people here will one day have time and will build little houses and love people of every colour; perhaps they will love permanence and hate transience and despise money. This country is a young heir of older countries. And the heirs have inherited before their elders were dead. Let the elders lie under the ground first, and then the young ones may become magnificent heirs.

'You must have patience!'

I, however, who am not a just man, don't have the virtue of patience.

I am a weak man, and I fear the Antichrist.

UNDER THE EARTH

I went to many other countries in the service of the master who had a thousand tongues at his disposal.

I descended eight hundred metres beneath the surface of the earth and saw men who for eight hours a day, eight hours on a daily basis, lie on their backs eight hundred metres under the earth. With hammers they broke off the coal over their heads, coal that is plentiful below the earth.

They are threatened by poisonous gases, by falling stones, by rocks that collapse suddenly and block the way out. And many workers had already died such a death.

God Himself made the coal form underground so that it may warm us, so that it may heal us, drive our machines and support the works of our reason.

But I also met people who deal in coal. And these did not lie on their backs for eight hours a day, eight hundred metres below the earth.

It is certainly true that God granted them the intelligence to trade just as He gave the others the strength and endurance to lie on their backs and hack at the coal above their heads.

The men who deal in coal can thus not be less in the eyes of God than the men who mine it.

Before God, I said, they aren't less. But before people, they *are* less, for their work is less strenuous and they earn more money.

Human justice is not as perfect as divine justice. People look at the degree of toil and the amount of its reward.

Every half-hour a lift brought the men below, eight hundred metres deep. When one is underground, eight hundred metres from the light of the world, one not only loses the light that illuminates the earth but one longs for the sky; one has nostalgia for the heavens.

We were not made as hamsters, moles, salamanders or worms but as humans; the earth is meant to be under our feet and the sky above our heads.

We were created to walk upright, on two legs not on four feet. Our arms and hands are not for crawling around the earth but for working, for embracing our neighbour and to stretch towards the heavens.

Through this also are we differentiated from the animals, in that we alone, among all the beings of creation, have the ability to stretch our arms and hands towards the sky.

We are also different from animals through the fact that our forefather Adam received the breath of God. It is as though we had been granted this power because we yearn for contact with He of whom we are a reflection.

When we descend into the earth, however, no more can we stretch our arms skywards. No longer can we create the symbol of redemption, the sign of the Cross, with our bodies while we stand. The Cross is not just the instrument of torture upon which the Redeemer of mankind suffered. It is first and foremost the simplest depiction of man with his arms outstretched, his feet planted on the earth, his head towards the sky. Every person on earth who stretches out his arms in distress forms a cross. He redeems himself, as it were, from his afflictions through the sign of the Cross, which he does not make but himself depicts.

Eight hundred metres under the earth, however, one cannot stand upright or stretch out one's arms. One creeps around like an animal, on all fours, through narrow, gloomy passageways. Water drips from the walls. Water and slime coat the hands and feet. The damp air paralyses the lungs and shortens the breath.

And one can plainly see that we were not made to be without the sky. Yes, when first we descend below the surface of the earth we understand that we cannot really live without the dome of the heavens over our heads.

It is because of this that miners refer to the heavy earthen ceiling that weighs down upon them, eight hundred metres deep, as the sky.

Men are so dependent on the sky that they would call a layer of earth eight hundred metres thick 'the sky'.

The word alone consoles them over the loss of the actual heavens.

It is the same as when emigrants who leave their old home and seek a new one in far-away lands give the names of their old cities and villages to the new cities and villages they found.

Our true home is the sky, and we are but guests upon this earth.

Under the earth itself, even when we descend eight hundred metres below, we never cease to feel that the heavens are our home, and that is why miners call the black ceiling above their heads the sky. Into this word they place all the blue sweetness of the true sky, as many people who have left their home sing to themselves a tune of their country, and all the sweetness of the homeland lives within this song.

But the men who call the ceiling above their heads the sky must work at it with hammers, picks and drills. They lie flat upon their backs and drill holes in their pitiful sky from which they collect coal. Sometimes this sky over them falls upon them and buries them beneath its black weight. Nevertheless, they still call it 'sky'.

It is not merciful to them. It is the most unmerciful sky one might imagine. It is a black sky.

The man who took me underground showed me his house. It was a Sunday. The man was old. For thirty years he had been descending into the bowels of the earth every day, eight hundred metres and even deeper. Each Sunday he spent at home, attending to his garden and his children. He had six sons. Five times he had been buried alive by a fall of coal and then rescued. Of all the companions of his youth none was still alive. They had all been crushed and killed by the black and merciless sky.

'And what are your six sons doing?' I asked.

'They are all miners,' he replied. 'My grandfather suffocated in the mine, my father also. I suppose I'll suffocate there, and perhaps also my children. But maybe they'll live to see the day when larger and safer tunnels are built. In that case, it will no longer pay to produce coal, as the prices are too low. Engineers are expensive. Once the safest tunnels are constructed, mining coal will no longer pay. Then the pits will be closed, and we'll have nothing to eat.'

'What leads you,' I asked him, 'to figure the lives of your forebears, your own and that of your children into the price of the coal that you don't even sell? Why do you think coal is more important than life?'

'I'm not saying that,' answered the man. 'The coal itself says so. We are prisoners of the coal. If it isn't sold, we all must die. If, however, it's sold for a good price, only one or another of us will die, but not all of us. That is why we reckon the price of our lives into the price of the coal, exactly as our masters, our breadgivers do. Just as they reckon, so do we.'

'Don't you love life?' I asked the man.

'I once came across a book,' he said, 'in which I read about and saw pictures of the ships of antiquity that were called triremes. These ships were rowed by slaves, each of whom was chained to his seat and had only one arm free – but it was the one with which he rowed. From time to time an overseer with a whip walked among the ranks of rowing slaves. And when one of them grew tired and didn't stroke the oar with enough energy he received a lash from the whip.

'Yet these rowers loved their lives anyway, just as the captain of the ship did or perhaps even more so. And they rowed with every last bit of strength to avoid a cliff, a rock or a storm, although they would have had nothing to lose if they had guided the boat against a rock or a cliff or into the middle of a storm.

'There was, kind sir, first of all the overseer's whip, and then the whip of the will to live, and the whip of the fear of death – three whips.

'Thus the slaves saved the ship and the lives both of their masters and of themselves. They did it because the ship's life was their own life.

'I, too – we, too – love life.'

And I took leave of the miner.

MANKIND IN CAGES

The Master of a Thousand Tongues also sent me to factories, to schools, to all locations where unrest might appear, to report on everything that was new and uneasy by investigating the origin of its unnaturalness.

I thus saw houses made out of glass and steel and chromium metal, not out of brick and stone. And I saw how each type of man built himself the house that fitted his own particular nature. In studying this phenomenon I realized that people change much more rapidly than other creatures.

Since the creation of the world birds have built their nests, spiders their webs, hamsters their holes, foxes their lairs and ants their hills, always in the same fashion. But men lived first in caves, then in huts, later in houses, and now they live in cages. In cages of glass and steel.

'Let the sun shine in!' they say. A saying that is as foolish as the sayings of which I have already spoken – *Religion is the opium of the people* and *Education is power*.

In a cave, in a hut or in a house one is not imprisoned. But in a cage one is imprisoned. It seems that at about the time that we began to rise up into the air like birds and to feel that we had shaken off the chains that bound us to the earth, we were just then punished with the longing to experience the unhappiness that birds sometimes suffer, namely to live in cages.

In a cave, a hut or a house of stone and brick a man is sheltered, but in a cage he is imprisoned.

The modern man, that is to say the man in whom the Antichrist has begun to work, says: 'Let the sun shine in!' – as if he were no longer capable of leaving his house to savour the sun whenever he wished.

Cages are made out of glass and metal bars because imprisoned animals cannot enjoy sun and air whenever they need it.

If man willingly builds himself a cage, he must feel like he is truly a prisoner. And even though he has the key to his modern cage he is still a prisoner.

But who is it that holds him captive and causes him to shut himself up in a cage apparently of his own free will?

The Antichrist holds him prisoner.

The cave, the hut, the house of brick and stone, they provide shelter and protection against storms, lightning and the fiery sun, enemies and dangers of all types. But the new houses of glass and metal are open, even when the doors and windows are closed. They are open and closed at the same time, as only cages can be.

There is no quiet and no solitude in such a house. In these homes, even silent light is noisy.

There, a fish could begin to shriek and a deaf mute to babble. Meanwhile, the man who has been granted the grace of speech – which is the breath of God – must be silent in these houses if he wishes to say something human to his neighbour.

And just as man is distinguished from an animal by the grace of speech he also has the grace of reticence, privacy and modesty. In these thin houses full of light and air there is no silence but, at best, a dumbness; no privacy but withdrawal and suppression; no modesty but, at most, shame.

When one enters such a building made of glass and stupidity and chromium metal there is one dwelling next to another just as one cage is placed next to another in the so-called aviaries of the zoological gardens.

So those people who have to live in such buildings are like animals and, at the same time, like homeless people. They spend the night in the street. And, still worse, the street spends the night with them. So it is as if each individual were spending the night with his neighbour.

The tenderness of two lovers in bed is as visible as the caressing of caged birds.

One could say that the sun, which has been let in, has brought everything into the daylight.

Those men whose job it is to build such houses say that they are practical and healthful. And, besides, people belong together. And, further, nothing human should be alien to people.

To these homebuilders, however, everything human is foreign. Solitude, silence and secrecy are just as critical to us as health, sun and fresh air. It is certainly inherent in our nature that we should live in a community with our own kind. However, we can only endure this community if we can also spend time alone. For this is human nature – we wish to be alone and also together with other people. It is written that it is not good for people to remain alone.

But man, the image of God, possesses one of the divine qualities – the ability to be both alone and with others at the same time. Yes, he has nostalgia for solitude, just as he has nostalgia for Heaven, because he was created in the image, that is to say, according to the characteristics, of God.

He cannot live in a community if he cannot satisfy his nostalgia. He disturbs the community instead of helping it.

It is only in the hour of danger – during times of war, for example – that people can stand the constant company of their own kind; and this is only because death is in the neighbourhood and death makes everyone lonely because it carries everyone off individually, even when it takes thousands in a single moment.

In the houses of which I am speaking, however, the people do not live in the face of imminent death. And they yearn for solitude.

But the designers and builders of these houses say: 'We have to give the poor shelter, not luxury. And solitude is luxury.'

Yet it is exactly when the houses are intended for the poor that one should remember one of the worst curses of poverty – that the poor man is unable to be alone. And it is better that he should occasionally go hungry than that he should never be able to break his bread alone.

Often he would rather be alone under the wide sky at night than with others under a roof. For, although it is not good for man to live alone, it is equally bad if he is forced to be together with others.

This, however, the architects and constructors of the new houses do not know.

So people today live like birds.

They can fly, and still they live in cages.

THE BLESSINGS OF THE EARTH:
PETROLEUM, POTASH, POISON

I came to one of the regions where oil wells are found. And I wrote from there to the mighty Master of a Thousand Tongues:

Mighty Master of a Thousand Tongues

I am in one of the most interesting of countries, where the famous oil wells are located. It lies at the base of a mountain range, and its activities are centred in a quite remarkable town. Oil has been found here since the mid nineteenth century. The dark wooden derricks rise from an area about fifty square kilometres in size.

They seem to me less cruel and, in a way, less dangerous to the earth's surface when I compare them with derricks in other countries – countries that bear upon their face that curse of barrenness that is like a counterpart to the fruitfulness that lies within them. Here in this town, the sun is moderate, and there are still forests that yield only reluctantly to the towers and seem to encompass them peacefully rather than flee from them in hostility. The eye can sweep from the covered wells to the green hills.

But there is dust, white and exceptionally thick. It is as though it were not the accidental product of waste and separated matter but an independent element like water, like fire or earth, and as though it were less like the latter than the wind by which it is swirled around in a thick haze. It lies in the street like flour, powder or chalk and envelops every vehicle and pedestrian, seeming to act according to its own impulse or instinct. It has a quite special relationship with the rays of the burning sun, as though it were its duty to complete the sun's task. And when it rains the dust transforms to an ash-grey, damp, sticky mass that coagulates in every tiny hollow into a greenish puddle.

So here is where oil is obtained. This city was just a village a couple of decades ago. Now about thirty thousand people live here. A single street – about six kilometres long – connects three towns, and it is impossible to tell where one ends and the next begins. Adjacent to the houses there stretches a wooden footpath made of short, sturdy stakes. It is not possible to build a pavement because the oil is carried to the rail station by pipes under the street. The difference between the level of the footpath and the carriageway, but also the little houses, is great, so that the pedestrian is as high as or even above the level of the rooftops and one can look down at an angle into the windows. All the little houses are made of wood. Only once in a while does a large house of brick, whitewashed and stony-faced, interrupt the sad rows of crooked, decaying and broken-down dwellings. They all sprang up overnight at a time when the stream of oil-seekers began to flow into this place. It is as though these planks had not been hastily pieced together by human hands but, rather, that the breath of human greed had accidentally piled up chance materials; not a single one of these temporary homes seems to have been meant to accommodate sleeping people but, rather, for the purpose of preserving and increasing the restlessness of insomnia. The rancid odour of oil, a stinking wonder, was what brought them here.

The incalculable illogicality, even from a geological perspective, of the laws of the underground, heightened the diggers' excitement to the point of lust, and the constantly acute possibility of being separated by scarcely three hundred metres from a fortune worth countless millions was bound to cause an intoxication stronger than that of possession. And, although they were all exposed to the unpredictability of a lottery or a game of roulette, none of them gave in to the fatalism of waiting that would gradually prepare them for disappointment. Here, at petroleum's source, each person indulged in the illusion that destiny could be dominated through work, and his passion in the search aggravated the dismal result into a disaster that he could bear no longer.

The small well-owners were only freed from the unbearable alternation between hope and discouragement by the powerful intervention of the large ones and of the 'corporations'. These could purchase several properties at the same time and wait on the whims of the subterranean element with the relative calm that is one of the manly virtues of wealth. Besides these powerful interests, for whom patience cost nothing and who could quickly sow millions in order to reap an eventual harvest of billions, there came speculators on a smaller scale, whose lower credit was balanced by smaller risk, and these diminished even further the chances of the working-class adventurers. These gradually gave up their dreams. They kept to their shacks.

Many wrote their names over their doors and began to trade – in soap, in bootlaces, in onions, in leather. They withdrew from the stormy and tragic domain of the fortune-seeker to the pathetic modesty of the small shopkeeper. The shacks that had been built to last a couple of months stood for years, and their provisional frailty became stabilized into a characteristic of local colour. They resemble the flimsy constructions of a film studio or the primitive book-cover illustrations of Californian stories or hallucinations. It seems to me, having seen many great industrial areas, that nowhere else does such a sober business undertaking take on such a fantastic physiognomy. Here, capitalism wandered into the territory of expressionism.

And it seems that this place will hold on to its fantastic nature. For the town moves – and not only in a metaphorical sense. As the old wells stagnate, new ones are opened, and the dusty street wanders towards the oil.

It shoves its little houses ahead, winds into a curve and extends itself zealously in the wake of the capricious oil.

So I can hardly give up the idea that this street will one day be endless, a long, white, dusty ribbon going over hills and into valleys, crooked and straight, temporary and yet permanent, short lived as human happiness and long lived as human desire.

I will admit to you that the appearance of this large town, consisting principally of a single great street, caused me to forget the actual conditions of its social order. For a time, speculation and the passion of money-making seemed to me elemental and almost mysterious. The grotesque faces of greed here, the persistently tense atmosphere, where frightening catastrophes could suddenly occur each day, at any time, awakened my interest more for the destinies that were suited to literary treatment than for those of the everyday. The fact that even here there must be workers and clerks, wage rates and unemployed, was often surpassed by the seemingly fictional quality of the individuals. Fantasy was more alive than conscience.

At any rate, the oil workers are incomparably better off than, for example, coal miners. They are skilled workers even here. The working conditions are relatively favourable. The men work in places that, while not airy, are at least not closed off from air, and the smell of the oil is by no means unpleasant and is even said to be healthful for the lungs.

To the layman, all the instruments that are used for boring appear to be disappointingly primitive. Motors drive the drills. A man circles continuously around a type of basin, holding an iron rod horizontally in his hand. As simple as his motions and activities look, they are in reality equally difficult. The experts say that the skill of a workman consists of his ability to feel by hand the degree and type of difficulty with which the drill meets, the low or high level of resistance offered by the rock. The worker's hand must therefore have a highly refined sense of touch and, in part, provide a substitute for the function of the eye, which in well-drilling is completely useless. If the bore hole is accidentally blocked by some object falling into it – for example, a large screw – ingenious and crafty methods are used to extract the blockage with the aid of instruments that grope around in the darkness before they grasp and remove it. Their endeavours remind one of attempts to bring to the light a cork that has fallen into a dark and narrow-necked bottle. Hours, months and money are lost on it.

Money, money, so very much money! Remember that boring to a depth of fifteen hundred metres costs about ninety thousand dollars. It is a lottery game for people who don't need one, for bankers, consortiums, and American multi-millionaires. The men for whom a fortune may erupt out of the ground here have already lost the ability to become happy through material gain. There is a distinct contrast between the fabulous way in which the earth offers its treasures and the stoical calm with which the shareholders of oil stock can await the coming of the miraculous event. These poor treasure hunters live somewhat removed from the scene of Nature's wonders, in the great cities of the West, and the fact that they are far away, invisible and practically impersonal, bestows upon them the brilliance of gods who direct engineers and workers through mysterious transmissions. Foreign financial titans own the great majority of the oilfields. The employees are paid from a kind of magically replenished chest. Somewhere in the distance, on the great international stock exchanges, shares are traded and transactions take place according to unfathomable laws. Astronomers are more familiar with the genesis and fading of heavenly bodies in space than are the managers and directors of oilfields with the changes in ownership of the wells at which they work. The minor officials can only sit and tremble as their ears perceive the reverberations of larger storms in the world markets. For example, three large enterprises were recently sold to a Western consortium. A small conference was held at one of the world's markets. Three or four gentlemen took out their fountain pens and scrawled their signatures on contracts. And here in this oil town five hundred officials were put out of work; starvation peered through their windows and was already raising the door latch, all because the Master of a Thousand Oil Wells had spoken a brief sentence: 'We are going to centralize!'

Sceptics claim that the new owners were only planning a stock-exchange manoeuvre, their purpose being simply to sell the shares at a higher price and not actually operate the wells.

The workmen head home with the same certainty that is only seen in peasants returning from work in the fields, and it is as though they carry the same scythes upon their shoulders that their grandfathers had carried before them. A few poor people stand at muddy pools of water and collect stray oil in cans. They are the lesser colleagues of the great Parisian Dreyfuss. They have no shares, only buckets. They sell their findings of oil in very small quantities and light with it their provisional wooden cabins. This is the entire share that they receive from bountiful Nature. Their shacks stand crooked, brown and resigned in the golden rays of the sun. They appear to be huddling ever closer to one another, trying to become smaller and eventually to vanish altogether. And tomorrow, perhaps, they will no longer exist.

I hope that I have given you an idea of the atmosphere of this eastern California. I have described it to you to demonstrate that it is not my intention to send only idyllic reports from this country.

Meanwhile, I remain

Your obedient servant

J.R.

I then came to a region where they manufacture poisons. These poisons can kill. But since everything on earth contains within it two sides, it is true that the poisons can also nourish. One of the poisons is called ammonia. Using this, they fertilize the earth and kill the enemies of the fatherland.

One of the others is called potash.

In this region there was a village that was visited one day by skilled engineers. They examined the fields and meadows and found that great quantities of potash could be obtained from the earth of this village.

They returned to the poison factory and reported to the Masters of a Thousand Poisons that there was potash in this village.

So the Masters of a Thousand Poisons sent clever agents to the village. These agents told the owners of the fields and meadows nothing about the potash. They simply offered them money, great quantities of money, for their fields and meadows.

The farmers loved their fields and meadows, but they loved money even more.

And thus they sold the fields and the meadows to the Masters of a Thousand Poisons but asked if they could live in their homes and on their land for ten more years.

This took place, however, a year before the great war that is known as the World War.

But once the war broke out there was a need for potash and also ammonia, not only to make the soil rich but also to bury the enemies of the fatherland under the earth and transform these enemies into rich manure. So the fields and meadows were taken from the farmers, although the ten years were not yet up – for what validity do the laws of peace have over those of war? – and with them was taken that which lay beneath, the potash.

A giant machine came, what is called an 'excavator'. This is a hellish machine that rips up mouthfuls of earth and destroys everything that grows or lives on the surface. And this machine destroyed the houses and farms, the barns, stables, ploughed fields and meadows.

In this village there also stood a church, in the middle of a cemetery. The peasants said they would not hand over their dead or the church, however much potash there might be alongside the bones of the dead. For they had not sold the churchyard to the Masters of a Thousand Poisons.

But the Masters of a Thousand Poisons paid money, more money. The dead were exhumed, one grave at a time, and they were transported to the next village where there was no potash under the earth's surface.

On a certain day the villagers gathered in the church so as to take their final leave.

While they were praying and saying farewell, outside, the excavator began to shake the ground. And the roof of the church collapsed, along with the bells, on top of four hundred people, and the cross was sent flying into the open potash pit. The bells were made into cannon and the four hundred dead were turned into ammonia. And with this ammonia the enemy could be poisoned.

I came to this village. It is no longer a village, it is one great wide pit of potash and ammonia.

A stench of pestilence and putrefaction dominates the air.

An old man, the caretaker, who had known the place when it was a thriving village and whose face was already marked by death, said to me: 'I often think of the old village. But the fact that it has died wouldn't trouble me so much if its constant heavenly guests were still here. When it began to stink of ammonia here, the birds vanished. Under this sky the larks trill no more. The swallows no longer build their nests in these parts. To say nothing of the storks. Even the ravens and crows avoid our area in winter. Yes, the sparrows have also left. For twenty years I haven't heard the song of a bird. If I had money, I would go far away so that I could hear the song of a bird once more before my death.'

So spoke the old man. And in the air the stench of plague and chemicals reigned.

In this region a poison called nitroglycerine is also manufactured. With this, houses, cities and mountains can be blown skywards. If any of this nitroglycerine is left over it is sent to a neighbouring factory where artificial silk and goods made from artificial silk are produced. There they make stockings for women, and from there came the stockings that the *doppelgänger* of her beautiful shadow wore when she made nineteen attempts at dying in Hollywood and showed her calves as she died. Her calves were clad in nitroglycerine.

POISON GASES ARE ONLY LITTLE CLOUDS

Then the mighty Master of a Thousand Tongues told me: 'Go and look at the battle pictures that people paint so that war is not forgotten in peacetime.'

And I wrote to him:

Mighty Master of a Thousand Tongues

The old battle pictures aren't terrifying; rather, they are touching. The bloody red that may once have predominated has become brick-red, even a bit carroty-red. The tattered flags flutter at the front of the battle. Indeed, they have been sliced by sabres, ripped by swords, pierced by bullets. But the very fact that these delicate fabrics of cloth or silk can meet deadly weapons and still survive many battles confirms the impression that wars in the old days were actually more harmless than they are portrayed in the history books. The presence of many fallen soldiers is undeniable. Their deaths don't appear to have been final. They still have time to let a curse escape from their lips before they die or to bless the cause for which they have fought. It is obviously clear to them, at the moment of death, that they will awaken by some miracle to a further cheerful life of war, or they already see the military part of Heaven that is waiting to receive them.

No wonder! The enemy is usually non-believers – Turks, janissaries, Tatars, whose religion is at its base monotheistic but which contains a fundamental misunderstanding. This is evident in their curved swords. Those who fight on our side – the Christian side – have straight swords (symbolic of the character of the warriors) with a handle that can at any time be used as a cross. While the janissaries, Tatars and Saracens prefer small, nimble, reddish horses, the heroes of the Occident ride on white horses reminiscent of the doves of the Grail. Ordinary men rescue the prominent heroes at the last moment. In general, the saviour is fatally wounded. But one already surmises that his descendants will receive a fief as soon as the hero's wounds are healed.

The battle usually takes place on a plain, the character of which is emphasized by the surrounding heights. On these hills stand the high commanders, those in whose name the battle is being fought. Behind them and out of sight most likely stand their white tents, in which the black-haired courtesans lie and keep their fingers crossed. If the battle goes unfavourably, those in whose name it is being waged are the first to turn around and go to their tents. They must be broken down in great haste. But the vanquished leader still has time for a fleeting embrace from his mistress.

It sometimes happens, however, that the hill – and what lies behind it – cannot be evacuated in time. In those cases, the victors storm out from the convenient plain, and the first of them to reach the top wave to those who are still below. Waving generally plays a great role in war. Somebody is always waving to someone else – to victory, to fame or to death. And those who wave apparently know very well that they are setting an example and that their actions will be handed down for posterity. The cause for which they are fighting and waving is a good one. The followers are aware of this, and they do not hesitate.

The sky is blue, the sun is hot and yellow, the dust white. The warriors' throats are dry, and the spectator thirsts even at the sight of the battle. The various wounds must cause fever and intensify thirst. It makes one want to carry a bucket of fresh water to aid the men who are fulfilling their difficult duty under the fiery sun. One would like to refresh the fighters. It is impossible! There is no spring near by and there are no buckets on hand! The viewer can take comfort in the thought that they will drink when the battle has ended.

As evening comes the battle ends. We know that the sunny part of the day lasts about twelve hours. As soon as the sun sets behind one of the hills at its disposal, the trumpets blow in retreat, even if the battle is not yet decided. The sickle moon climbs slowly over the horizon and reminds one of the curved swords of the enemy. The unharmed lie down to sleep. And the wounded begin to groan.

There is nothing more horrible than the fact that the *last war* is already becoming the subject of idyllic war paintings. After it has ceased! Particularly in the victorious countries, where the people imagine that they have won the war somewhat in the same fashion as the knights of Christendom once vanquished the heathen. The poison gases seem like neat little clouds whose destructive force is a guarantee of resurrection.

The little cannon spit forth their lovely little flames. The little aeroplanes hum swiftly through the breeze. Touching little field postcards are written by heroes to their sweethearts. Especially beloved is the storming of trenches. Just like the attacks against the Saracens! Occupied hills are stormed with bayonets. These attackers are caught in barbed wire that pierces their entrails. And someone waves! Someone waves! To victory, to fame, to death!

Yet we are still alive. We, the Saracens and the Christians. And we notice how they paint us, our fathers, our younger brothers. They make films about us and paint war pictures to hang on walls, so that our grandchildren will again develop a blood lust. Before our own living eyes they portray our entrails. They are already trivializing our own deaths. They are already making field-marshal hills out of our corpse-hills. Only about ten years later. Ten short years! They are rebuilding so soon! And they are painting! . . .

But the red that they now employ – and this is our only miserable consolation! – will never take on the peaceful shade of brick. It will be red, red as blood and fire. Our blood, our fire. The colours of today are composed of a different substance than they used to be. Actual blood is mixed into them. And our deaths were the last deaths that may be enveloped in idyllic lies. The deaths of our painters will be different, not to be painted. They will suffocate in their homes, in their studios, with their palettes in their left hands and their brushes in their lying right! . . .

This, Mighty Master of a Thousand Tongues, is my reflection on battle pictures.

Your obedient servant

J.R.

P.S. Where shall I go now, Mighty Master of a Thousand Tongues?

VENGEANCE IS HIS

The Master of a Thousand Tongues sent me to the people who are scattered among all the other peoples of the earth – namely, to the Jews.

It is written that this people will be dispersed among all the peoples of the earth. Thus they have no land of their own. And, if one wishes to seek them out, one does not know where to go. Everywhere we see Jews among us. Where should one go to see only Jews?

The Master of a Thousand Tongues said: 'Go there, where the Jews live together, tightly packed into villages or small towns.'

So I went to the Jews.

And there I met people who were Jews, that is to say, all the world around them called them Jews. But I saw no difference between them and other people, except in certain traditions of everyday life and of religion.

And I wrote to the Master of a Thousand Tongues the following letter:

Mighty Master of a Thousand Tongues

As I have already had the honour to tell you face to face that I do not feel able to remain in your service, I allow myself now to inform you that I am unable to view the Jews to whom you have dispatched me as a people distinct from the other peoples of this earth.

I repeat to you, Mighty Master of a Thousand Tongues, on this occasion that I am not at all able to distinguish between peoples or send you reports that will make the people to which you belong believe that this people or that is different or remarkable.

I view all the people of the world to be remarkable but also equally average.

I hold that, above all, people are people. And as long as it is not viewed as an obvious truth that throughout the world and in all languages of this earth all people resemble one another much more than they are dissimilar, I think it is a sin to call out the differences between the various peoples instead of their similarities and commonalities.

Certainly there are differences between races and peoples.

These differences are, however, in the first place not as great as the differences between people who belong to the same race or nationality.

Second, they are much less pronounced than the similarities and equalities that unite people with people and race with race, such that I believe I would be doing God Himself an injustice, and therefore committing a mortal sin, if I were to emphasize the peculiarities of any one people instead of its similarities with all other peoples.

For all peoples descend from Adam, into whom God breathed His living breath.

If I were to make distinctions between the Children of Adam, I would therefore be saying that God breathed not one but many different breaths to create *different* types of peoples.

And, above all, I see in every person the image of God.

Respectfully, your obedient servant

Joseph Roth

And the Master of a Thousand Tongues answered me with the following:

Dear Friend

Do not write to me the things I already know either about yourself or about others.

Observe the Jews for yourself, with your eyes. This is all I ask of you.

Your

Master of a Thousand Tongues

So I began to visit the Jews.

And I saw that above all they were regarded as quite a special people as their womb gave birth to the concept that says the peoples of the earth, the whole earth, are all the Children of God.

Because they were the first to say that all people of all nations are equally the Children of God, it is now said that they, the Jews, see themselves as the special Children of God.

For so it is in this world, where the Antichrist prevails for the moment, that the people who say they want good will be accused of evil.

The ancient Jews said that they were God's chosen people.

But to what end did they say this?

To the end of bearing the Saviour, Jesus Christ, who died on the cross for *all* the people of the world.

The arrogance of the Jews was, therefore, in reality humility.

They were not chosen only because – as we know – the redeemer of the world came from their womb, but also because they brought forth the only Son of Man of whom it is *not* arrogant to be proud. And they humbled themselves and even did penance for what was falsely deemed their arrogance by the fact that it was they themselves who crucified the fruit of their womb.

They knew that a crown had been given to them, but they trampled it with their feet.

They not only bore the Saviour; they also denied Him. They really were the chosen people of God. They were doubly chosen but not simply because they hardened their hearts and did not admit that the Son of God was the redeemer of the world.

The Jews were doubly chosen because they both brought Him forth *and* denied Him. They, the Jews, were chosen to bring forth the Saviour and through their denial make him into a Saviour.

Through their virtue as through their sin have they prepared for the redemption of the world.

Of their own free will they took the burden of sin on to themselves, as sometimes a father will do who does not wish to share in the fame of his son.

Therefore, whoever believes in Jesus Christ but hates, or even has low esteem, for the Jews, his earthly womb, is the brother of the Antichrist.

The heathens still honour all the places where their saints and prophets revealed themselves in their human weakness.

The false Christians, however, despise or hate or esteem lightly the womb of the Saviour – the Jews.

For the Jews are the earthly womb of Jesus Christ.

Whoever thinks little of the Jews, thinks little also of Jesus Christ.

He who is a Christian esteems the Jews.

He who hates them or thinks poorly of them is not a Christian and mocks God Himself.

For since the Jews were chosen to bring about the earthly death of Jesus Christ, through it they confirmed the covenant of God with Abraham, the covenant with which the redemption of this world began.

And if God chose the Jews not only to bring forth Jesus Christ but also to deny Him, it was because God Himself struck the Children of Israel with blindness.

And He himself may continue to strike them. He alone. Vengeance is His, and His also is the object of His vengeance.

Whoever attempts to take their own vengeance on the Jews in the name of God as His representative on earth is presumptuous and commits a mortal sin.

And whoever, in consideration of the fact that he is baptized and the Jews are not, tries to take vengeance against the Jews when, in fact, vengeance belongs only to God, is a twofold sinner. For he appropriates for himself, through the grace of his baptism, the authority to execute vengeance. He reveals the fact that the heathen yet lives within him, the heathen who does not deserve the grace of baptism.

He who hates the Jews is a heathen and not a Christian.

He who can hate at all, whomsoever may be the object of his hatred, is a heathen and not a Christian. And he who believes that he is a Christian solely because he is not a Jew is twice and even thrice a heathen. Cast him out of the community of Christians!

If the Church does not cast him out then God Himself will cast him out.

The Jews whom I saw in the villages and small towns of Eastern Europe are no different in character or nature from other people.

That is to say, I saw in them no special characteristics other than that which we already know, namely that the sexual organs of the male Jews are circumcised.

I saw Jewish farmers and Jewish craftsmen, Jewish traders, Jewish soldiers, Jewish artists, Jewish poor and rich, Jewish nobles and Jewish commoners, satiated Jews and hungry Jews, destitute and wealthy Jews.

And I saw other men around who were not Jews, and they said: 'The poor, the rich, the satiated and the hungry, the soldiers and the artists, the traders and the craftsmen – they are all Jews. They don't believe in Jesus Christ.'

'They don't believe in Jesus Christ,' I said to them, 'but *you* are even worse, for *you* believe in a *false* Jesus Christ *who is made in your image*.

'You are unjust.

'You thus have an unjust Jesus Christ. You thirst for vengeance and blood. Therefore you have made for yourselves a vengeful and bloodthirsty Jesus Christ. You have been baptized, but you aren't Christians. It is true that you have received the grace of baptism. It will, however, only become reality after your death. So long as you live on earth you act like heathens. For I see with my own eyes that the unbaptized Jews work, get hungry, earn money and lie or tell the truth as you yourselves do. They love and they hate; they conceive and give birth; they make music and pursue many other arts; there are shoemakers and tailors among them just as there are among you.'

'But they are more clever than we,' said the people.

'Even if they were more clever than you,' said I, 'that would indicate not only that you envy their intelligence – and envy is a sin – but also that you cultivate their intelligence through oppression.

'Your envy is so immense that you not only gratify yourselves by feeding it with the already existing objects of your envy but you are zealous to supply it constantly with new nourishment!

'Perhaps (but you've never tried it) the Jews would be more

thick-headed than you are if you gave them the opportunity to be just as foolish as you and yet live as you do.

'Since, however, you treat them unjustly and even oppress them, you develop their intelligence and thus also the object of your envy.

'You are possessed by the Antichrist.'

Thus I spoke to the people.

But they replied: 'How is it that we are possessed by the Antichrist when we are fighting the Antichrist among the Jews; among the Jews, where he alone still feels that he fits in and is at home?'

I said to them: 'The Antichrist is at home not among the Jews but among you. And not only *among* you, but *in each and every one of you*. You yourselves are the Antichrist. It isn't just that you hate someone; you make the objects of your hatred worse than they were so that you may hate them still more.

'I see no difference between you and the Jews who live among you unless it be that it was from the womb of the Jews that the Saviour was born.

'And were it so that I knew you envy the Jews because they were the Saviour's womb, I would consider it a good excuse.

'But it is not so.

'You envy the Jews because they earn earthly goods. This is the truth.

'You wanted all the earthly goods for yourselves. The Antichrist is among you and in you.'

I continued to go among the Jewish people, and all that I saw confirmed my conviction that there were good and bad among them, just as their faith delineated holy days and ordinary days.

And in a small town I witnessed one of their holy days, the highest of them all, the Day of Propitiation, or Atonement, which they call Yom Kippur.

Yom Kippur, however, is a day not of Propitiation but of Atonement, a solemn day, the twenty-four hours that contain twenty-four years of penance.

It commences on the previous day at four o'clock in the afternoon. In a town where the majority of the residents are Jews this greatest of all holidays is felt like an oppressive storm when one finds oneself on the high seas in a frail boat.

The lanes were suddenly dark because the candles in all the windows were blown out, and the shops were closed hurriedly and with timid haste but at the same time with such an indescribable finality that one believed they would not be reopened until Judgement Day.

It was an all-encompassing absence from everything worldly, from business, from joy, from nature, from the streets and the family, from friends and acquaintances. Men who two hours earlier had been going about their daily business with their accustomed expressions hurried as though transformed through the streets towards the temple, wearing heavy black silk or the dreadful white of their shrouds, with white socks and loose slippers, heads bent forward, their prayer shawls under their arms. The profound silence, in what was usually an almost orientally noisy town, seemed to be increased a hundred times and weighed heavily even upon the normally animated children.

All the fathers blessed their children. All the women wept in front of silver candlesticks. All friends embraced each other. All enemies begged one another for forgiveness. A choir of angels sang out to Judgement Day. Soon Jehovah opened the formidable book in which the sins, punishments and fates of the year are laid down. Lights burned for all the dead; others burned for all the living. The dead were separated from this world and the living from the here-after by only a single step.

The great prayers began. The great fast had already begun one hour before. Hundreds, thousands, tens of thousands of candles burning in a row and one behind another, bent over and mingled flames as they melted together. From a thousand windows erupted shouted prayers to be interrupted by nearly silent, low other-worldly melodies that seemed to echo the singing of Heaven.

People stood shoulder to shoulder in all the synagogues. Some threw themselves upon the ground, rose after a long period, sat down on stone tiles or footstools, crouched for a time and then sprang up suddenly, shook their upper bodies and ran continually to and fro in the small chamber. Whole houses, ecstatic outposts of prayer, were full of white shrouds, of the living who were no longer here, of the dead who were now alive. Not a drop of water crossed those dry lips to refresh those throats that were crying out so great a lamen-tation – not into this world but, rather, into the heavenly world. It was dreadful to think that no one would eat or drink, either on this day or the next. They had all become ghosts, with the characteristics of ghosts. Every small shopkeeper was a superman, as today he desired to reach God. They all stretched their hands outwards to grasp at the tip of His vestment. All, without distinction; the rich were as poor as the truly destitute, for none could eat. They were all sinners, and all were praying. A frenzy gripped them, and they swayed, they rested and whispered, they beat their breasts, they sang, they shouted out, they wept; heavy tears ran down their venerable beards, hunger was forgotten amid the grief of the soul and the eternity of the melodies heard by the enraptured ear.

I asked the people who lived in the area and hated the Jews or held them in low esteem whether they had noticed the Jews' God-fearing and devout nature.

And one of the righteous of whom I enquired, who was himself a Jew, said: 'Do not believe the wicked people around us who wish to destroy us, but neither should you believe the liars and the wicked among us. There are hypocrites in our midst – and people become not better but worse when they are haunted by hatred and misfortune. Many fear God's punishment, and that is why they pray. And others would like to entice God to give them some reward, and so they pray. Some cling to life and fear that in the coming year they will be struck from the Book of Life, and they fear death, so therefore they pray. And I know some who, as soon as the sound of the shofar becomes audible, signalling the end of the Day of Atonement, hurry to their full tables more avidly than they had hurried one day earlier to the set tables of God. For they are human and require food and drink. But there are others who hasten even more rapidly to their evil occupations and wicked thoughts, more rapidly than to their full tables. They do so because they believe that with a day of fasting and atonement they have pacified God, so that He will, so to speak, close an eye to their damnable deeds. Thus it was among the ancient Jews, our fore-fathers, that there were some who believed that with a little sheep or little lamb they could buy the right to sin. They didn't want to appease God but, praised be His name, they wanted to bribe Him. Such people are even more cursed than those who would deny Him, for they create a god in their own image and the qualities they assign him are not human but diabolical. And this is the greatest of sins – to worship God so that He may be more lenient towards injustice. May He protect us from that!

'But vanity and arrogance are also at home among our people.

I was at one time led by various misfortunes to celebrate our Day of Atonement in a distant city in the west of Europe. And, as the Jews of that town recognized me as a man of pious reputation, they requested that I lead them in a few prayers – so I did this. They prayed in a large and beautiful hall, the walls of which were adorned with all kinds of paintings and statues. And since our faith prevents us from making pictures and statues – for it is written that man shall make no images beside that of the invisible God, praised be His name in all eternity! – I asked how these adornments came to be in a synagogue.

'So they told me that this hall wasn't actually a house of prayer but had only been rented for the High Holy Day. For the Jews in this big western city didn't pray each day or each Sabbath, as do our Jews, but only on the High Holy Days. It wasn't worthwhile for them to pay the cost of having their own synagogue. "Certainly," I said, "certainly. For one can worship the Lord everywhere – and every place where He is invoked is a holy place. But He should be called upon every day – and one should spare no expense when a house is needed in which to give him praise."

'"In our country," said the other, "the people are different. Business, you see, business takes up a great deal of our time. And one must earn money! Alas, if only there were no such thing as money!" said the man, sighing and raising his eyes Heavenwards, as if pleading with God to abolish money.

'"If there were no such thing as money," I said, "you would invent it."

'"No!" he cried, "May the Lord protect us from such a thought!"

'I left him standing and continued to pray.

'In the evening, when the shofar had been blown and the people were heading home, I saw in front of the entrance two large

143

and gaudy placards, and there was a desk beside the door. Behind the desk I saw a pretty, made-up cashier girl selling tickets. And many of my co-believers, with whom I had been praying, approached the girl and purchased tickets for themselves. They said they were just going to have something to eat and would return shortly. And so it was. They went to the inns, where they ate and drank, and then returned. In the room where three hours earlier they had been praying and fasting, yes, in the very same seats, they enjoyed the spectacle of shadows rushing and scurrying hither and thither across the screen. And the man with whom I had just spoken invited me to be a guest in his house the next day, so I went there and saw that his house was that of a rich man. I saw that God had granted him prosperity – and I respected him for it. Then I asked him about his business. At that point he smiled and said: "I own the large theatre in which you prayed yesterday. I am first to buy the top films in the world. There are more than fifteen hundred seats in my theatre. The hall is well ventilated. In the summer it is kept cool, for I have a cold room under the floor and about a hundred ventilators. On the High Holy Days I rent the theatre for divine worship. And I wouldn't even accept payment but would lease it for nothing, if only money didn't exist!"

'"Then I recognized that I had dealt with the Evil One himself. I had prayed and eaten in his house. So I left him on the spot.

'And yet,' finished the righteous Jew, 'he was a very pleasant man. He had a gentle glance and an agreeable voice.'

This was what the righteous Jew recounted to me.

Thus I realized that the Antichrist dwells also among the Jews, just as he does everywhere else. And he is already sitting in the synagogues just as he is sitting upon the spires and crosses of the churches.

THE IRON GOD

I received a message from the Master of a Thousand Tongues that I should return to him as soon as possible.

I had already, he said, visited many nations and cities, so now I was to take a holiday, see my own country and do anything I pleased.

So I visited my own country, that is to say the land of my Master of a Thousand Tongues.

This country lies in the centre of Europe, between east and west, and is a remarkable country, that is to say, many of the people who live there seemed to me remarkable. Many among them boasted that God had chosen them. And when I asked one of them for what purpose God might have chosen them, he said: 'To place the world in its proper order, to grant it the light of our thoughts, the richness of our language, the truths our scholars discover practically on a daily basis.'

'Everything that you mention,' I replied, 'can also be achieved by all the other people and nations of the entire world. Nobody has ever been chosen by God to perform earthly deeds, unless such deeds are in service of Heaven. He must be a remarkable God.'

'He is a remarkable God. He is our God. Our own God. The God of our nation. The God whom all others worship is the God of Love, a pitiable creature. But our God is strong. He is the God of vigour. He made the iron grow. He is an iron God.'

'You worship,' I said to him, 'not the golden calf but an iron one.'

'We don't worship,' said he; 'we fight, and that is our prayer.'

'So you fight not only against the other peoples but also against the God of the other peoples?'

'Yes,' he replied, 'and we have never yet been defeated.'

'Then,' I said, 'continue your fighting. But you are already defeated even before the fight has begun.'

But he did not understand me so dismissed me abruptly.

And as I left his house I saw a man standing in front of his door with the sign of the Cross on the cap that sat over his forehead and upon his right arm. But it was no ordinary cross, rather, one on which the right and left, top and bottom ends were broken and bent. It looked as if the man had first wantonly broken the holy symbol of the cross and then forgotten the right way to put it together again. It also seemed that the cross itself suffered pain in being so crooked and deformed. And as I felt pity for the man and also for the cross. I said: 'Kind sir, you've got your cross wrong. May I show you what a cross should look like?'

'No,' he said, 'my cross is correct. It is through this symbol that we shall conquer and not by the one that you have in mind.'

'You're mistaken,' I responded.

The man then hit me over the head so that I collapsed on the ground and lay for some time as though dead.

Then charitable people lifted me up and took me to a hospital.

And once I recovered my senses some time later I wrote again to the Master of a Thousand Tongues in the following words:

Mighty Master of a Thousand Tongues

I cannot visit in your country, for people beat me over the head and leave me for dead.

But this alone would not prevent me from seeing the country so long as I could hope to regain my health.

Other things hinder me, namely, the fact that in your country they have other gods than the One God. I was once in a land where it is said God does not exist. And in another land where He is seen as their rich uncle. And among heathen peoples who said there are many gods. But never have I seen a land in which people worship God and revile Him in a single breath. And where they not only do not follow the Son of God but even hate Him; and not only hate Him but even despise Him, His death, His love and His humility. For they have deformed His cross and say that it is the right and true cross and that it is not deformed and bent. Their God is an iron God. I know that it is written in the Revelation of John that the servants of the Antichrist would receive a mark in their right hands and on their foreheads. In this country the people already bear this mark. And they are preparing for the end of the world, but I cannot speak justly of them because they beat me on the head. Where one denies God, He may yet one day be acknowledged. Where He is unrecognized or unacknowledged He may yet reveal Himself. But where He is blasphemed and worshipped in a single breath the Antichrist is revealed. When the Children of Israel worshipped the golden calf the Ten Commandments had not yet been issued. Now, however, the children of your country are bowing before an iron calf five thousand years after the Ten Commandments were handed down and two thousand years after the Cross first shone its light over the world. Release me from your service now, Mighty Master of a Thousand Tongues.

His reply ran:

I dismiss you as of this date (date of postmark) from my service.

You are a refractory tongue. I have already found a new and more willing one.

My time, our time, has dawned.

I no longer need to treat you courteously.

So now I can close with the truth.

Hail the Anticross!

Signed

The Master of a Thousand Tongues

PEOPLE FEAR EACH OTHER

So I left the land of the Master of a Thousand Tongues and crossed the border into other countries.

I took up residence in one of the houses that they call hotels.

And there came all kinds of people who had known me when I was one of the thousand tongues.

There came a rich man, a poor man, a pious man, an unbeliever, a Jew, a Jew-hater, a heathen, a Christian, an agent of the Master of a Thousand Shadows, one who hoped for a world revolution and another who wished to maintain the world just as it is, one who wanted peace and another who desired war.

They had all read the truths that I had written. They came, some to question me, others to listen to me and a third group to corrupt me. And through all of them spoke the Antichrist.

Thus I sat each day – and thus I still sit today – in the hotel.

Many people seek me out, and all of them are convinced that I believe them and their words. However, I am protected by my fear of the Antichrist and am on my guard against the false words of my guests, even of those who are honest.

For sometimes they think they are speaking the truth when, in fact, the words belong to the Antichrist.

They themselves don't know it. But I can understand. For just as I myself, when I was a soldier, sold my shadow to the Antichrist without realizing it, so have they unwittingly sold their words to the

Antichrist, and out of their mouths come not the words themselves but what the Antichrist has transformed into the shadows of words.

Sometimes my visitors arrive together, the strong and the weak, the rich and the poor and so on.

And they offer one another their hands. However, they hate each other.

They would like to kill one another, but they talk with each other. And their words are so full of falsehoods and poison that it is worse than if they actually did kill one another.

They speak on friendly and murderous terms at the same time. It is the tongue of the Antichrist; it is their mother tongue.

The language of the Antichrist has become the mother tongue of mankind.

And instead of dreading the Antichrist they are afraid of one another. The poor fear the rich and vice versa, the Jew fears the anti-Semite and vice versa and so on.

For just as love and justice spring from fearlessness, so comes hatred from fear and injustice from fear.

Fear, however, is the daughter of the Antichrist. By this I mean man's fear of his own kind.

The lion does not fear the lion, the tiger does not fear the tiger, the lamb does not fear the lamb, the ox does not fear the ox, the raven does not fear the raven, and the carp does not fear the carp – when one does not threaten the other. Fear can only emerge between one and another creature of the same species if there is hostility between them for some reason.

But people fear other people without cause; in fact, the fear people have of each other is not the consequence but the origin of their hostilities and wars. Animals fear humans. They fear them more than they fear their natural foes among the other animals. The strongest of the four-legged beasts of prey fears a snake's venom, but both the serpent and the beast of prey fear man equally.

Since he is to be feared by all creation, man may truly be the master.

But, since he is also afraid of his own kind, he is thus not the absolute Lord of Creation.

If man were not afraid of his own kind he would have no fear of the tempter, of the Devil, of the Antichrist.

The Antichrist plants people's fear of other people into their hearts so that he may not himself become weak.

He sows fear. And from this seed sprouts discord.

As one person fears another individual, so does one nation fear another nation.

And within each nation each of the individual citizens fears the other.

And as soon as all the individual members of a nation fear a neighbouring nation more than the individuals fear one another, war starts.

The soldier who goes to war fears his superior, but the superior and the soldier both fear the enemy, that is to say, the other nation, even more.

Therefore, there will never be peace in the world so long as the fear of men towards other men exists.

Similarly, the fear of God cannot grow in the world as long as man fears man more than he does God himself.

Truly, the Antichrist sows man's fear of his own kind to prevent him from fearing God.

Fearing God, that is to say, not only loving God but also loving each other.

To fear man, however, is to hate man, to abandon God and to be in the presence of the Antichrist.

And this is the condition of the world today.

We are further than ever from the hour when the predator will befriend the prey.

Not even man can befriend his fellow man.

All the animals of creation fear humans. But people's fear of one another today is even greater than animals' fear of people.

For man knows frightfulness of his own kind better than animals.

This is the hour in which, as it is written, man is worse than a ferocious animal.

THE TEMPTERS

A man who claimed to be righteous came to me and said: 'I come from the country where the Master of a Thousand Tongues, in whose service you have been, lives.'

'Aren't you going to return?' I enquired. 'They are lacking in righteous men there!'

'They drove me out,' said the false righteous man, 'and others with me. In all other countries of the world righteous men are downtrodden and must suffer. But in this country they are banishing justice entirely. They are seating wrong upon the throne of right. They are removing the bandage from the eyes of Justice.'

'So they are finally allowing her to see?'

'No,' replied the just man, 'they aren't removing the bandage so that she can see. Although even that would be false. For it is the nature of Justice to judge without seeing. Her delicate hands, which measure and weigh, are surer than the eye. She has to apply not the judgement of the eye, visual justice, but the scales, the judgement of the hands, manual justice. Truly, when Justice can see, she *ceases to be Justice*. But the unrighteous haven't removed the bandage from her eyes to let her see! They have removed it in order to make her blind. *They have poked out her eyes.*

'At that point the righteous left the country.

'Yet we cannot abandon Justice, although we, the righteous

have been driven out. And we endeavour to act justly towards the country that blinded her.

'I have long wondered why these people poked out the eyes of Justice. And I believe I have discovered the reason: the people were acting foolishly, not wickedly. By no means do they understand the nature of Justice. From the beginning they had feared that she might one day take off her blindfold and see. And, as fools are impatient, they anticipated her. But when they saw her eyes they were terrified and pricked them out. They are poor fools.'

'So what do you ask of me?' I enquired of the just man.

'That you should be just towards this country,' he replied. 'That's why I've come to you.'

'I bow before your sense of justice,' said I, 'but I cannot myself be just. I am a man. I have fear of the Antichrist – I will try to take vengeance on him. And the Lord Himself will one day decide whether I am worthy of salvation.

'I respect the just man. But I am not great enough to understand him. I am only an ordinary man. I fear evil. And I hate it.'

At this, the man who thought he was righteous left me, and clearly he resented me.

And when I asked myself why he resented me more than he did the unjust people who had driven him out and blinded Justice it awakened in me the suspicion that the Antichrist was also working within and gnawing at the supposedly righteous man.

I confess that since this meeting I fear even righteous men, those who are too just, those who want to understand everything and those who say they can forgive everything.

There certainly exist men of that sort. But people who can both hate and love and who hate hatred and love love – these are men of my kind.

For I fear that the Antichrist hides himself even behind the man who is all too just, whose righteousness is false.

There next came to me a man who called himself unjust. He spoke to me with pride and said: 'I am but one of the many millions of unrighteous men; an anonymous unrighteous man, but of that I am also proud. Soon, I will be even less of a name than I am today, for the number of the unrighteous grows with every hour, and soon there will be countless billions, like ants.

'I, too, come from the country of the Master of a Thousand Tongues, in whose service you once were.

'I come because I saw that you were visited by my enemy, our enemy, the righteous man. What he told you was lies and falsehoods. I come to tell you the truth.'

I replied: 'Since you yourself say that you are unrighteous, how then can you accuse a righteous man of doing unrighteous things?'

The unrighteous man said: 'A change has recently come to the world. It is now such that the unrighteous are right and the righteous are wrong. I therefore wish to inform you that you are unjust when you say that the righteous man is right.

'For you must remember that there are only thirty-six righteous men in the whole world but millions of unrighteous – and soon there will be billions. How can thirty-six poor individuals continue to be right against billions? Would it be just if thirty-six men were able to continue in the right against billions?'

'Right is right,' I retorted, 'and wrong is wrong, and numbers have got nothing to do with it.'

'How has right ever prevailed except by force of numbers?' asked the unrighteous man. 'Many thousands of people one day acknowledged that this was right and that was wrong, and ever since that day there has been such a distinction.'

'No,' said I. 'It is always individuals who have handed down laws and proclaimed what is right – Lycurgus, for example, and Moses and Muhammad and Jesus Christ. For right is divine, and God chooses not a thousand spokesmen at the same time but only one, and it is by this that we recognize that right and justice are divine. For example, as is customary, numbers decide the election of a beauty queen but not who is the goddess of justice. There may be some who say that the queen of beauty isn't beautiful enough. For the choice was decided by numbers. And whenever numbers alone decide something, there are always some, more or less numerous, who have a different opinion. But, when God decides, there can be no disagreement. Beauty is a matter of taste, but justice isn't. When, however, justice is decided by numbers it is injustice.'

'But individuals can also err!' said the unrighteous man.

'When they err,' I said, 'their law is arbitrary. It may be that thousands or millions or even billions see this despotism as right and just. However, these thousands and millions and billions only do so because arbitrariness is disguised as justice.'

'It is true that God proclaims His justice through the mouths of individuals. But *this* justice is alive in all men without distinction. They don't know what it is called or how it will appear before it is proclaimed, but they have innate knowledge of its nature, and they have already prepared to receive it.

'It is true, and in this respect I must admit that you're right, in this world sometimes one expects a guest named so-and-so, but there comes another who calls himself so-and-so, and he is given the reception that has been prepared for the real guest, since his hosts don't realize that he isn't genuine. But the impostor always calls himself authentic, the thief honest and the murderer a lover. He who wishes to pass off a lie as the truth calls himself a truth lover. The murderer comes in the night with sweet words and begs entry. The unrighteous man speaks of righteousness – as you have, in fact, just done to me. Why don't you say that your unrighteousness is wrong? Why do you call it right? Why don't you say that numbers make might, instead of saying that they make right? Because you want to corrupt me!'

'You do me wrong,' said the unrighteous man. 'For one of the demands of justice is that numbers should decide. If, for example, ten men are not of *one* mind, the issue in question is put to a vote. And if seven are for and three against, these three follow the seven.'

'Yes,' I said, 'if ten reasonable and just men come together, then the vote is just. But if nine fools are brought together with one wise man, the wise man is right and the nine fools are wrong. A vote can only be taken among equals. And just as you cannot add together two apples and four fish so you cannot sum together the votes of two wise men and four fools. It is true that two and four are always six. But only when the numbers two and four represent objects, animals or men of the same kind.'

'So thirty-six men can be in the right against billions?' asked the unjust man.

'Of course. Even one man can be in the right against billions.'

'Then you shall be made to feel the power of the billions,' the unjust man said menacingly.

'And afterwards all these billions will feel the power of right!' I retorted.

And he departed in discord because there was no other way for him to leave.

*

Next a weak man came to me, one of those who are today the most helpless victims of those in power, namely, a Jew.

'I come to you,' he began, 'because I have just seen my enemy, the unrighteous man, go through your door. And I must tell you that the powerful are unjust. They torment the weak. They say that a majority really equals right and justice.

'They violate and mock not only the law of hospitality but also the law of humanity.

'The law of hospitality is itself a mockery of humanity.

'For what kind of world is this where it first had to be established by a special law that one man is a host and another a guest? Wasn't it God who gave us houses? And if God gave no house to a particular man, may he not reside in the house of his neighbour, which is also the house of God? Let us, however, admit this: that whoever owns a house may be proud of it and may also be proud of offering friendship. We Jews also had a home once. But for us it was written that the stranger in our house is to be treated as a fellow countryman. And all among us observed this command. Yes, we even passed on this command to the strangers. And they learned when they were with us – although they quickly forgot – to offer hospitality, which is better than receiving it.

'Now, however, they say that we aren't worthy of their houses.

'Are these then their houses and their lands? Is man therefore a tree that he cannot move from place to place? And don't we transplant trees so that they grow in other countries? At what point in time does a people begin to regard this or that country as its own? Hasn't every people taken its land from another people? Did it buy land? If I deprive my neighbour of his property, does it become mine after ten, a hundred or a thousand years have elapsed? If the former owner returns after a certain period, do I have the right to expel him? Only He who has given also has the right to take. And since God Himself gave countries to the peoples but none to us, is it not He Himself who sends us to the various countries that belong to Him and Him alone? Have we, perhaps, sinned more than the owners of the countries? Suppose there were really hosts and guests – that God was not the only host and all men were not His guests – have we faulted more than our hosts? And isn't a fault a fault just as a virtue is a virtue, regardless of who has faulted or who is virtuous?'

'God has allocated the houses,' I said, 'and also homelessness. He has granted justice – and also injustice. He has granted reason and also stupidity. Someone who has reason, as you do, and yet demands justice on earth, is wrong. If you had a country of your own, would you accept the people who came to visit you when they no longer had a country and not require greater virtue from them than you demand of your own kind? And, if you are of the opinion that God gives houses and countries, you must also know that He alone gave your people the Law. He alone made the Jews powerless. And He alone made men unjust. Because you have suffered so much injustice do you wish to inflict still more injustice on others? When you see injustice perpetrated upon a Jew, are you pained by the injustice alone, or are you doubly pained because it is a Jew who is suffering?'

'Both,' said the weak man.

'If that is so,' I replied, 'it might happen that you will one day become a cruel man. You carry the seed of injustice within you.

'On what grounds therefore do you come to me and complain about it?'

The weak man left me with a sigh, but it sounded like a curse. He sighed and cursed at the same time. By this I recognized that he also, this weak man, was commanded by the Antichrist.

The ability to sigh came from God.

But the curse within it came from the Antichrist.

*

But then those who hate the Jews sent me one of their own.

'I am a hater of Jews,' he said. 'I call myself an anti-Semite. The Jews plague the world with their breath, their businesses, their minds, their books, their songs, their pictures and their faith. They are bloodthirsty and goldthirsty. They are power-hungry and vengeance-hungry.'

'I have no reply to that,' said I. 'I have seen many evil men. But their wickedness was a human wickedness, for man is weak and is inclined to be evil. Their own earthly wickedness was mixed together with just a grain (or sometimes a few grains) of that wickedness that I recognize as the hellish evil of the Antichrist.

'But out of you, anti-Semite, there speaks the entire wickedness of the Antichrist. For you live upon the hatred that all other men in this world also know but which they don't all act upon – hatred towards the Jews.

'You are filled completely with this hatred and with this alone. And you have even less trouble than other zealots do in spreading your hatred among mankind.

'For, as I have said, you find in all the people of the earth the smouldering spark of this special hatred.

'You see, all other haters have at least to make some effort to light in the hearts of other men the same fire than burns in their own hearts.

'But you put a flame to a common one that is already smouldering in most people's hearts.

'You are therefore unlike the average arsonist who takes the trouble to lay the match in the barn or the village and seek out and prepare the kindling.

'You are a lazy arsonist. You light fire where a spark already glows.

'You aren't an arsonist because of your own human love of a fire. You are a helper of the Antichrist.

'It is he who fans the spark. And you are with him, in his service as an incendiary. You don't work because of your own wickedness; you work by order of the mighty evil of the Antichrist.

'I have seen many evil men, but in each of them there was still a certain degree of chivalry, that human characteristic from which, even when love and goodness have died, there is always the possibility that justice may grow. With you that is impossible.

'There are, however, weak, evil men who hate the evil men who are strong and all other evil men as well as good men and weak men.

'He who hates only those at whom the spark of hatred is directed, the spark that already glimmers in everyone's heart, is worse than an ordinary hater – he is a hater without chivalry.

'For the Jews are hated by the faithful and the godless, the oppressors and the oppressed, the healthy and the sick, the rich and the poor and, as they say these days, the capitalists and the proletariat, by those who say all men are equal and others who say that all men are not equal, by white people and by coloured people.

'But if it happened that I was inspired by a desire to hate, I would find people to hate other than the Jews. Furthermore, you must acknowledge the remarkable fact that all, without distinction, don't like the Jews – even if they don't hate them – and this should make people realize that it is God himself who has struck the Jews with the hatred of mankind.

'God alone has the right to punish the Jews. He, God Himself, hates people who hate the Jews.

'Certainly the Antichrist lives and works among the Jews as well. However, he who hates them alone causes everything else, everything else of which the Antichrist has taken possession, not to be hated.

'By this I also recognize that it is the Antichrist who drives the anti-Semites. He chose them so that all the other evils that he has instigated remain undetected.

'The Antichrist works like an illusionist. While he waves his magic wand with his right hand he is already holding in his left hand the magic surprise that he said he would conjure using his wand.

'You, anti-Semite, are the right hand and the magic wand of the Antichrist. You make all the wickedness of the Antichrist invisible while his left hand is conjuring up the Jews.

'You are the disguising magic cloth and the lying handkerchief of the Antichrist.'

The anti-Semite then left me. He resented me. Alas, I was proud that he resented me.

Then came another righteous man whom the Antichrist had corrupted and persuaded to visit me to convince me to believe that he understood the anti-Semite.

This and that evil – said he – had the Jews committed. One must understand.

At this, I told him that it isn't the concern of men to understand wickedness when a wicked man explains it. One cannot understand the anti-Semite when an evil man calling himself an anti-Semite argues that the Jews are wicked.

'Overall, it seems to me,' I said to the righteous man, 'that these supposedly noble words "to know all is to forgive all" had been coined by the Antichrist himself.

'It is the privilege of God,' I said, 'to know all and forgive all. But just as the Antichrist has convinced man that he possesses other divine qualities, so has he convinced him that he can know all and forgive all.

'So, for example, a man can fly. But one day he might fall headfirst.

'He isn't an angel; angels don't fall. Even birds don't fall.

'A man may also believe that he knows everything. Still, he can suddenly fall headfirst from the heights of his reason.

'His reason is fragile, like an aeroplane. He cannot know or forgive anything.

'That is the privilege of God and of the thirty-six true righteous men.

'Their identities, however, we don't know.

'And if we do happen to recognize one of them, who knows whether he isn't then removed from the thirty-six as though he had died?'

This false righteous man also resented me and left.

Thereupon the Antichrist sent another man, who came and said: 'I love my country. Allow me to introduce myself. I am a patriot.

'In my fatherland any evil may be perpetrated, perhaps even committed against me. I love it anyway.'

'If evil is committed in your fatherland,' I replied, 'and you still love it, then you don't love your country but, rather, evil itself.

'If good is done anywhere, I love the country in which good is done.

'Where it is good, there is my fatherland. That isn't to say that wherever things go well for me is therefore my country.

'Rather that is to say that *wherever there is good, there is my home.* And a home where good isn't done is no home at all.

'Above all, we are Children of God, and God alone is our home. He has given us legs and feet not only so that we may be at home in all His countries but also that we may leave a home where evil is perpetrated. Where evil is practised is *not* our home.

'*That* is why God has given us feet, so that we can leave a home where evil is perpetrated.

'Whoever stays in a home where the people sin against God doesn't deserve to have feet. He doesn't deserve to call God his home. God is our only home. In His sublime presence there can be no evil but only love and justice.

'Outside of His sublime presence He has given us no home other than paradise and after that the entire earth.

'The whole earth is *temporarily* our home. Our real home, however, is the eternal presence of God.'

At that the patriot also left me resentfully.

Then a pious man was sent to me, a man of the Holy Church, who wore a brown robe, a cord around the waist and a large cross.

'Praised be Jesus Christ!' he said.

'In all eternity, Amen!' I replied.

'I see,' he began, 'how you are fighting against the Antichrist. I will bring you help. I come from Rome, the holy city. I am one of the most humble servants of the Holy Father. But I have the honour to stay often in his hallowed environs.

'I once saw another sitting in the place of the Holy Father on the throne of Peter.'

The monk was silent for some time. Then he reiterated: 'Someone quite other!'

I, too, was silent for some time. Then I said: 'It is written that a time will come when the Antichrist will sit upon the throne of Peter adorned with all the insignia of the office of the Holy Father. Tell me, is this time already come?'

'I don't know,' replied the monk. 'I am but one of the lowliest servants in the palace of the Holy Father. One day, however, I saw that the Holy Father had fallen asleep.

'He was asleep for just a few hours.

'But in this time another sat himself upon the exalted throne.

'And it happened that precisely during these hours ambassadors from a number of heathen counties came to make their peace with the Holy Church.

'There were three countries, three different countries. But the ambassadors of each of these lands said nearly the same thing, and the first ones said: "We render unto God the things that are God's and unto the emperor those that are the emperor's. You, Holy Father, have only to say yes. And we shall have prayers said in the churches and praise the name of the Saviour. In return, however, we beg you, Holy Father, to bless our emperor."

'The ambassadors kneeled, the Holy Father was perched high upon his throne, and all around stood the cardinals, all in their prescribed ornament.

'And they all took that Holy Father for the real Holy Father. I alone knew that he, the Holy Father, had fallen asleep.

'I wondered how he could sit upon the throne of Peter and converse in such an amicable fashion with the ambassadors of the heathen.

'The first of the ambassadors said: "We wish to conquer only half of the world, Holy Father, not all of it! This half of the world once belonged to mighty Rome, so why not us? We are the heirs.

'"We only want to shoot, Holy Father, only to shoot a bit.

'"We want no more, Holy Father, than to stab, to stab just a little, and to wear the daggers that are required in order to stab.

'"But we also promise to pray, Holy Father. We will also pray.

'"We will honour you, Holy Father! You shall have an automobile from the best manufacturer in our country. And an apparatus called a telephone, fashioned of gold and ivory. And all the Edisons, all the Edi-sons, all the sons of Edom, will dedicate their inventions to you. We will take you to see the world, Holy Father, in special trains and in special automobiles. We shall keep all the holy days and have our children taught the precepts of the Saviour twice weekly; but seven times a week, only seven times, we will teach them to shoot and stab."

'And then the ambassador of the second country spoke. "Holy Father, in all Christian humility, we want not half the world but all of it.

'"But this also only in the name of God the Just.

'"Rome once ruled half the world. But we have conquered Rome. Therefore, the whole world belongs to us.

'"Allow us, Holy Father, to vanquish the entire world.

'"In return for this we shall pray and guarantee that we won't torture any more priests, for we are of the Germanic race and don't willingly torture when we are promised that which we demand.

'"We also wish to shoot and stab and wear daggers, and twice a week we will have our children learn the precepts of the Saviour.

'"But only seven times, *only* seven times in a week, will we stab and shoot, Holy Father.

'"But even this we shall do in the name of the Saviour.

'"We will acknowledge not just *one* Cross but two.

'"One on which the Saviour died. And the other to which we have made a few modern adjustments. We call it the crooked cross.

'"Let us, Holy Father, have four hooks on our cross!

'"In return, we shall destroy the godless, demolish the Jews, sanctify Sundays with shooting practice and offer up a prayer before each shot."

'And the Holy Father nodded.

'Then the representatives of the third country came forward. They said: "We come from Hollywood, what some call Unholywood, but you shouldn't believe them, Holy Father.

'"We no longer wish to conquer the world, *for we have already conquered it.*

'"We are the Land of Shadows.

'"Goldwein-Mutro-Mayer sent us.

'"Goldwein-Mutro-Mayer and its associates bind themselves to disseminate the shadow of the Saviour on to all the screens of the world.

'"We shall make up your genuine cardinals and your genuine priests using the techniques of our art, so that they may become genuine shadows.

'"In this way we will be able to spread the genuine faith across the world, through use of genuine shadows.

'"For this we desire your blessing, Holy Father, and also your own holy shadow.

'"And Goldwein-Mutro-Mayer, mightier than the powers with whose ambassadors you have just spoken, wishes also that we might bring back a concordat.

'"For the purposes of propaganda.

'"For Goldwein-Mutro-Mayer doesn't see why we, the Holy Trinity and rulers over the shadows, should have less than the rulers over the bodies, who in reality only desire to kill.

'"Whereas Goldwein-Mutro-Mayer kills *nothing but shadows.*"

'At this point, the Holy Father nodded.

'And he concluded a concordat with Goldwein-Mutro-Mayer and its associates.'

This is what the monk related to me.

'I don't believe you, Brother!' I said.

'You're wrong! The Holy Father has not fallen asleep! The Antichrist is not yet sitting on the throne of Peter!'

At this, the monk grew uncertain and said: 'I am truly only a humble servant in the palace of the Lord. To err is human!'

Whereupon I said to him: 'Get out! The end of days hasn't yet arrived.'

He went obediently and fearfully. And it seemed possible to me that even he was the Antichrist or a messenger of the Antichrist.

But before long I became certain that he really was a messenger of the Antichrist.

For in the evening, in one of the theatres that they call cinemas, I saw my own shadow.

The Antichrist had filmed me while he was speaking with me, the enemy of the Antichrist.

Amid the shadows of skiers, rowers, tennis players, boxers, actors, politicians and criminals he also showed my shadow.

He had robbed me of my shadow.

So I left the theatre.

Also published by Peter Owen

FLIGHT WITHOUT END
Joseph Roth
978-0-7206-1068-0 • paperback • 144pp • £9.95

PETER OWEN MODERN CLASSIC

'Almost perfect.' – *Rolling Stone*

'A concise, powerful writer who brilliantly evokes the social, political and intellectual turmoil of the era.' – *Publishers Weekly*

'A novelist whose major novels deserve a wide readership.' – *Sunday Times*

Flight Without End, written in Paris in 1927, is perhaps the most personal of Joseph Roth's novels. Introduced by the author as the true account of his friend Franz Tunda, it tells the story of a young ex-officer of the Austro-Hungarian army in the 1914–18 war, who makes his way back from captivity in Siberia and service with the Bolshevik army, only to find that the old order that shaped him has crumbled and there is no place for him in the new 'European' culture that has taken its place.

Everywhere – in his dealings with his family, with society, with women – he finds himself an outsider, both attracted and repelled by the values of the old world, yet unable to accept the new ideologies.

Peter Owen books can be purchased from:
Central Books, 99 Wallis Road, London E9 5LN, UK
Tel: +44 (0) 845 458 9911 Fax: + 44 (0) 845 458 9912
e-mail: orders@centralbooks.com

www.peterowen.com

Also published by Peter Owen

THE SILENT PROPHET
Joseph Roth
978-0-7206-1135-9 • paperback • 220pp • £9.95

PETER OWEN MODERN CLASSIC

'A novel one should not wish to be without . . . Roth is a very fine writer indeed.'
– Angela Carter, *Guardian*

'With Roth's strikingly elliptical style, which can evoke despair through real wit, it would be only mildly flattering to view him as a compassionate, laconic Conrad.' – *Time Out*

'No one since Pasternak has captured so well the dreadful benevolence of the Tsarist tyranny.' – *Independent on Sunday*

The Silent Prophet is the result of Joseph Roth's visit to Moscow in 1926 when speculation about the fate of Trotsky was rife. Roth reffered to this work as his 'Trotsky novel', but the experiences of the book's hero, the Trotsky-like Friederich Kargan, are as recognizably those of a less well-known Jewish outsider, a perpetual exile searching for a place in the new Europe that emerged from the Great War and a set of values to counter his own scepticism and growing disallusionment – Joseph Roth himself.

A beautifully descriptive journey from loneliness into an illusory worldliness and back into loneliness, *The Silent Prophet* is a haunting study in alienation by a master of realistic imagination.

Peter Owen books can be purchased from:
Central Books, 99 Wallis Road, London E9 5LN, UK
Tel: +44 (0) 845 458 9911 Fax: + 44 (0) 845 458 9912
e-mail: orders@centralbooks.com

www.peterowen.com

Also published by Peter Owen

WEIGHTS AND MEASURES
Joseph Roth

978-0-7206-1136-6 • paperback • 150pp • £9.95

PETER OWEN MODERN CLASSIC

'An absorbing fable, dark, beautifully written and with a physical immediacy in the prose . . . I want to read more.'
– *New Statesman*

'*Weights and Measures* gave me the purest reading pleasure . . . A haunting little book, touched by genius.' – Robert Nye, *Guardian*

'Written with the melancholy wit and grace of Gogol . . . passages of electrifying beauty.' – *The Times*

At his wife's insistence, Eibenschutz leaves his job as an artilleryman in the Austrian army for a job as Weights and Measures Inspector in a remote part of the Empire near the Russian border.

Attempting to exercise some rectitude in his trade duties, he is at sea in a world of smugglers, profiteers and small-time crooks. When he discovers that his wife has become pregnant by his own clerk, he spends less and less time at home, preferring to frequent a tavern on the border. Here, he becomes hopelessly drawn to a beautiful gypsy woman; she, however, is prepared to share the bed of the landlord Jadlowker, Eibenshutz's enemy, an unprincipled profiteer who has made the tavern a beacon for local smuggling activity.

Peter Owen books can be purchased from:
Central Books, 99 Wallis Road, London E9 5LN, UK
Tel: +44 (0) 845 458 9911 Fax: + 44 (0) 845 458 9922
e-mail: orders@centralbooks.com

www.peterowen.com